INTRO

A BEGINNER'S LOOK AT THE ART AND CRAFT OF THEATRE

Thaddeus L. Torp
Professor Emeritus of Theatre
Central Connecticut State University

Nibsi:
Who always made the
art and craft a joy.
Your Caesar of the upside-down
crown,
Thaddeus L. Torp
Jan 1997

"It is the glass of truth --"
The Scarecrow by Percy Mackaye

KENDALL/HUNT PUBLISHING COMPANY
4050 Westmark Drive Dubuque, Iowa 52002

Publications translated and edited by the author:

Ibsen: Ghosts, and Strindberg: Miss Julie.

Strindberg: Ghost Sonata, and Ibsen: When We Dead Awaken.

Credits:

Theatre drawings by: Lani Beck Johnson

Chapter Headings by: Timothy Johnson

ISBN 0-7872-2784-6

Printed in the United States of America
10 9 8 7 6 5 4 3 2 1

Table of Contents

To the inspiration of my students
and their rekindling love for
scholarship, artistry, and craftsmanship.

"We were seeking the light..."
Pelleas and Melisande by M. Maeterlinck

INTRO

Preface

This little book intends to be no more than its title would suggest: abbreviated. No pretense here at giving you a complete in-depth coverage. That would require volumes, and the accompanying course would last for years. There are, however, certain basic facts and concepts regarding this subject which allow a suitable framework for lively discussion and study. I have collected these in order to give you a beginner's look at this phenomenon called Theatre.

Theatre is usually classified as a fine art form. This suggests that various aesthetic principles can be applied to it, and their emotional responses in its observers and practitioners can be analyzed. This will be part of the purpose of this book. At the same time we should recognize that theatre is often taught as a skilled profession. This implies that there are craftsman-like approaches to the doing of it which can be acquired. This aspect will be studied as well.

Then, too, Theatre is often approached merely as a historical entity: an accumulation of names, dates, books, and buildings which have survived the passage of time and somehow come to represent moments of note in that passage. Though I do not intend to present this as theatre history, I have made some use of those events momentous to proper understanding of what theatre has come to be. And I have made use of the historian's chronological form for much of the content of this text.

It is my hope that this small volume can guide your understanding of all of the above notions. It should at the very least supply you with a reference manual to the many ways man has found to look at this very human endeavor which he has labelled: Theatre.

UNIT I

The Theatrical Experience: Fundamental Terminology
Where do we begin our study?

"It's only a game, after all."
Hay Fever by Noel Coward

Chapter One
Definitions: What are We Talking about?

Theatre
Theatre happens whenever individuals isolate themselves from a group in order to perform a story for it. In Theatre language the individual performers have come to be labelled **actors**, the isolated area a **stage**, the group an **audience**, and the story a **play**. Each of these nouns has particular resonances worth examining.

The 4 Nouns

The word **actor** carries within it the implications of activity or doing. It has also come in some instances to suggest feigning or falsifying. Many modern actors prefer to be seen as artists of "being" rather than of "acting" and try to impress their viewers not with a performance but a living moment. It is important to remember however you see him that the actor is a necessary element of the theatrical performance. This always necessary human presence makes theater of all the fine arts the most humanistic. Another popular word for actor is "thespian." This title comes from the name of the famous Greek actor of the 5th Century, B.C., Thespis. His countrymen credited him with many innovations in playwriting and performance and his name became the catchword for his profession.

Stage is a word that also suggest artificiality to some readers. A structure of some sort that stands the actor off from his audience but at the same time makes him easier to hear and see. Men have developed a wide variety of staging methods over the centuries and their cultural and artistic solutions are a study in themselves. A course in Theatre must view these structures and the varied ways used by actors to relate to their audiences. Like "thespian" the word "theatre" also originated with the Greeks. The "theatron" or "seeing place" was where the spectators were seated to observe a play in performance. Thus our generic term has been assumed from what was only a part of the physical staging in the 5th century.

Audience is a word that originally implied only hearing as "spectator" implies only seeing. But as the actor must both be seen and heard to make a complete performance so both sight lines and acoustics have always been a concern of the theatrical stage. Two other features of the word audience will be vital features of our understanding of theatre. First of all it is necessary to remember that in theatre "audience" is always a collective noun. A theatrical performance requires more than one auditor to qualify. One spectator will only observe a rehearsal, but two make it a performance. This is true because a theatre production involves of necessity a give-and-take of a multiple nature that is not required in the other arts. Secondly, the theatre in any historical period bears the weight of a number of conventions of performance which its audience makes use of to interpret what it is experiencing. Without an understanding of these expectancies we cannot hope to view the theatrical event to which they contribute.

Our fourth noun, **Play**, gives us most difficulty when the time comes to justify a serious study of theater. "Are you still fooling around in the theater at night?" my mother once asked me in all seriousness. I was, of course, a college professor at the time; but I was "putting on a play" after normal business hours! This capricious title for the story essential to a definition of theater also carries an understanding of the active sense of all theater. A play is not just for reading but for enacting. To use the word "script" would imply only written words, while "drama" is a word that most English and classic departments have traditionally used to describe their predominantly literary approaches to story line. "Play" then will do.

Theatre then for our purposes is defined as: an actor performing a play to an audience from a stage.

The verb

The only verb in this definition is "performing" and it is present tense and active. Theatre is an art form that is experienced as it occurs. It is participated in at the same time by both the actor and his audience. And, it involves both a giving and a receiving.

Art

It is not as easy to define the word Art. Nor to lay out the ways in which theater fits within it. Art has always been viewed from two seemingly non-compatible perspectives. On the one hand it is a skill or a craft to be learned and practiced by artisans. (i.e., the art of cooking, the art of diving, the martial arts). It reaches out over a broad range of learning when it gives itself to part of the designation: Liberal Arts. Theatre, however, is more specifically classified as one of the Fine Arts. These, which include music, dance, painting, sculpture, poetry, etc., are further distinguished by the application of aesthetic judgement. Theories of beauty and skills of utility are both inherent in the word. And both aspects combine in theatre to produce a continuing tension that is at the heart of the lively theatrical event. For unlike the other arts theatre exists only in practice. It is always in the process of honing its own improvement. And the achievement of this is always in the process of being judged even as it is experienced by its collective audience. You judge it at the same time that you experience it. And your judgement (applause, laughter, coughing, indifference) contributes to the shaping of it.

Theater then has some unique characteristics and some that it shares with other arts. The play itself, or script in this case, shares with poetry and creative writing the aesthetics of language use, diction, word play, symbolic meaning, figures of speech. However, these are actively employed in the theater not merely dormant for analysis on a page. With the dance it shares a use for movement for pleasurable or emotional impact. Dance and theatre are the only art forms which require a human agent in their presentation. Along with music, theatre shares the fourth dimension. It can only exist as an event that encompasses a passage of time.

I have already stressed the point that theater requires a collective response. Add to this the fact that more than any other of the arts it is a collective endeavor. Although the actor is the most obvious artist in the theatrical event (and the only truly essential one in our working definition) his performance represents a coming together of the skills and sensibilities of many artisans. So theater then is an art form that requires elements of language, activity, humanity, time, and illustrates both a group effort and a group response.

Aesthetic judgements also require an analysis of emotional responses. Here theatre shares with the other arts the general and current notions on what is pleasing, what is fearful, what is amusing. It requires one response which is not only necessary but unique to it. This emotional ingredient is **empathy**. Spectators and performers alike must enter into a shared understanding of the story being enacted. Only with this imaginative projection can a series of events became dramatic in the truest sense of theatre.

Theatre history

The history of theater is very old, but the study of that history is very young. Though we date our Western theater tradition from the 5th century, B.C., only in the present century did we begin to study it as a cultural factor. Play scripts, of course, had been collected haphazardly more as examples of eccentric taste during past eras than as representations of a living and viable art form. They were studied usually only for their literary merits or shortcomings. The buildings in which these plays were performed were retained often only by sheer accident and then were studied mainly as structural examples rather than for the understanding of the events which occurred within them. Actors, of course, have been continued curiosities of their time. But often notoriety rather than talent or contributions led to a remembrance in a historical sense.

The task of an introductory course must include a bringing together of these elements from different disciplines in order to reach an understanding of this complex history. The most ephemeral element of all in this study is the audience. What were their experiences? We must understand their contributions if we hope to understand the theater in any given era. And like many historians we must continuously analyze how we have come to know these things.

Theatre history then will be covered in the ensuing chapters through a combined view of the literary tenets (play), the production methods (actor, stage), and the conventional perception of the spectators (audience) in each age.

Reading

And now a cautionary note to keep in mind as you read the supplementary plays essential to your understanding of theater. Remember first of all that these were performed art, not merely literature. Try to envision the action and re-action they elicited. Also bear in mind that many are translations from another language. They bear, therefore, the stamp of an additional artist's sensibilities. They cannot completely sound like they were intended to sound.

Some are outright "adaptations" in which case the script has often been altered not only in content, but often in tone. It is also helpful to remember that prior to the 19th century, stage instructions, cast lists, and interpretative notes were not put into the printed text by the playwright. Things as rudimentary as "enter" or "exit" and even identification of characters speaking lines were not a part of many early plays in written form. What we read, then, will be open to interpretation. But that of course is what theatre and this book are all about.

The Woman uses a table for a stage to address the assembled workers and in so doing acts out her own martyrdom. This scene from Toller's **Man and the Masses** illustrates the definition of a play. In this Expressionist drama the setting is a metaphor for the threatening world of the machine age looming over all in overpowering proportion. The massed workers are costumed in robotically similar work clothes except for the Old Woman and Young Girl stage right and the Foreman by the table, all of whom are given characterizing lines of dialogue. Note also the exposed theatrical lights.

Chapter Two
The Play: What is it telling us?

Story

Putting aside for awhile the other three nouns of our definition let us take a closer look at the Play. What are its characteristics and in general how does it differ from other literary forms? We know already that we experience it in a different manner: by having it acted out for us. But just what is it these actors are presenting to us? An audience is impressed by the **story**. And the story of a play is judged on how "**dramatic**" it is. Critics and audience members alike gauge the success of plays on the basis of this characteristic. We need, therefore, to investigate both of these terms to see what conclusions we can reach about them.

Plot

A story is first of all a string of events. It has a beginning (prologue or introduction) a main course of action (development) and comes to a conclusion (resolution or denouement). This structure is usually referred to as plot. The elements of a plot then are a person, an action, and a result. Each of these function in a particular way in dramatic structure.

Many people define plot as conflict. It involves a confrontation of opposing forces, and this is what makes drama. But all conflict is not necessarily dramatic. We must become involved in the struggle and its probable outcome for that to be true. In other words, the audience must empathize as we have learned. The Greek word for this struggle or conflict was **Agon**. From this word are derived the terms **protagonist** and **antagonist** by adding the prefixes "for" and "against". Even though we may not necessarily be "for" or "in favor of" that person's goals we still call the central character of a play the protagonist.

As for the action central to the play this may not be a conflict between individuals so much as an inner development in one character. It must, however, be capable of illustrating action or progression to an audience. And it must involve a human interpreter.

The conclusion of the story of the play is often referred to by the French term **denouement**: a tying together, resolution or outcome. Again this suggests that the story of the play requires an ending. certain questions must be answered in order for the play to reach a satisfactory wholeness in the minds of the audience. And as an audience member you should be able to tell the plot of the play you have experienced. Let's see how this might work.

Plot Sequence: ______________________________ is the story of
(Title of Play)

______________________________ who because
(Protagonist)

______________________________ sets out to
(Source of Conflict)

______________________________ with the following results
(Action of Play)

______________________________.
(Denouement)

Note that the action needs a spark to set it off. This can be referred to as the **inciting incident**. (What is the event in the play that starts the conflict rolling?) As you will see the way the audience has come to view these elements of structure has varied widely in history, but essentially plot has held a predominant position in our way of looking at a play. We will analyze this audience view more completely in the next chapter.

Theme

Some people feel that more important than the story line itself are the implications of that story. What is the meaning behind the plot? This is usually labelled the **theme**. Theme can be approached like plot in several different ways. It can be a broad generic term such as: a play about women's rights, or a play about misogyny, or an anti-divorce play. Sometimes the theme can be expressed as a moral statement (i.e., the play expresses the belief that only a good woman's love can save an erring husband). Some playwrights have felt so strong a need to justify their moral intent that they have allowed characters in the play to express the theme directly in the dialogue. These characters are given the French name: **Raisonneur**. Usually however the play in its action and resolution allows the theme to impress its argument on the audience.

Some plays have survived historically only because of the universal nature of the major argument or moral statement. This **universality** which also pertains to character development is important to our understanding of the play as much as our ability to follow the story line.

Character

Let's take a look then at the human agent whose actions become the story. The theatrical term for him or her is **character** and what differentiates one from another in any play is called characterization. The actor must present this character's persona to the audience using words or actions given or implied by the play. His methods will concern us later. For now our concerns are the methods of the characters' originator: the playwright.

Early playwrights made heavy use of stereotypical behavior. Their audiences, especially in comedy, expected this typification with only a few not very daring embellishments. The wife in these early plays is always taken for granted to be a shrewish nag; the father, a lecherous tightwad; the doctor, a user of big words even he cannot understand. Using the same word as our expression "stock in trade", we call these **stock characters**. Merely stating the character's name or seeing the costume or uniform worn by the actor could serve to differentiate them to their audience.

The playwright's means

Where more subtle variations of personality were required by the playwright only two means were at hand: words and actions. Unlike the novelist, the playwright cannot reveal omnisciently the inner working of his characters. He can only demonstrate these qualities and assume that his audience will interpret his intent correctly. Of course, the success of this also depends heavily on the actor's ability to illustrate these same intentions. Historically a number of devices have been used to try to overcome this impediment and present an omniscient voice. Early plays sometimes opened with a prologue spoken by a neutral personality who laid out the truth of the circumstances and very often stated the results to be expected from the story line. Still, coming at the outset of the play as it did, the observations of this all seeing character could be easily superseded by the events of the play.

Within the play itself characters had two methods of revealing inner thoughts. In **soliloquy** a character alone on stage could impart his motivations or even work out a thought process out loud. When other characters were present on stage he could voice an **aside** or motivating exclamation ("Now I've got him!" or "Heavens! That's my wife!") that was intended to show the audience the true thoughts of the character. A character was even invented for the very purpose of allowing the central characters to have someone to tell his or her thoughts to. This neutral individual is called a **confidante**. Despite all of these methods most modern audiences accept a truth about each character that they arrive at by what that character does and what he says. Less obviously of course comes what others say about him and how they react to him. Dialogue and action in its two forms.

Elements of differentiation

If he cannot tell us the truth about a character just what can the playwright tell us? 1) He can tell us and illustrate how the character sees himself. 2) He can show how the character wants others to see him. and 3) he can show how these others actually do see him.

But remember the only methods he can employ are those we also use in every day life: action and words. In the play as in everyday decision making it is true that the former weighs heavier than the latter in forming our opinions. What a person does is more important that what a person says when it comes to formulating our opinions of character. And in a play, where action is essential to story, the actions attributed to a character by the playwright become all important elements of differentiation. Words and speeches are merely secondary.

The conditions of the play are also important in formulating an audience opinion of a character. What are the circumstances under which the character is speaking or acting? Who is present or absent when this occurs? If it is merely reported on by a third party what emotions does this messenger betray? Are additional motives suggested? The theatre, like real life, allows us to experience character change and development. Those characters that do not alter during the limited course of the play are called static characters.

Levels of Characterization

It is possible to dissect a character and analyze the layers of meaning a playwright has given to it. But remember that secondary source material cannot prove this out. Modern playwrights and scholars of the ancients persist in penning lengthy essays to be appended to the printed copy or the programs passed out at performances. You, the audience, would make your decisions about characters just as you did on the story on the basis of lines and actions in the script itself.

The most obvious level of differentiation of characters is the surface layer: the **physiological** level. In everyday life we judge and categorize people we meet and deal with on the basis of rudimentary physical appearance. The theater also tends to deal in these same generalizations where characterization is involved. Factors of age, sex, ethnicity, physiognomy, size, grooming, and appearance can determine the way an audience initially views a character. Of course historical era as well as the national background of the audience can alter judgements as to what is beautiful or ugly, what pitiable or admirable, etc. The play may not be specific at times: Is the servant a man or a woman? Old or young? Attractive or homely? Or, on the contrary, it may specify the sort of physicality that is essential to the workings of the play: She is old enough to be his mother. Only men fought at the front. No one but an invalid would feel trapped in this tower. Sometimes historical knowledge inherent in the audience's background make factors inevitable: Helen of Troy was beautiful. Henry VIII was fat. Joan of Arc was a young girl. This level of characterization is usually left to the actor and costume to put across, but sometimes the dialogue in the play is used to enhance or undercut its effect on the audience.

We should remember that although in real life appearance is the least meaningful way of judging human nature, in the theater generalities are a part of the artist's tools and these appearances and their meaning must be taken seriously. If the playwright suggests that everyone on stage is repelled by the sight of a character, if a character has to put a big book on a chair to sit comfortably, if he comments over and over on the velvet jacket worn by a character it must be assumed there is a reason. If the dialogue describes a character as beautiful each audience will decide what that means and judge the performance accordingly.

Beyond the purely physical level a playwright can utilize **sociological** factors to differentiate his characters. What is the individual's background? Are details of his or her childhood brought up in the play's dialogue? Is the character educated or trained in any way? Does the script specify a profession or trade? Prior to the modern period playwrights and their audiences took much of this sort of detail for granted. A crowned head or a servant's livery would automatically explain behavior and speech patterns. Modern man has come to regard heredity and environment both as necessary tools to understanding human actions. So sociological details are a necessary factor in modern plays.

More important than these surface factors are the **psychological** levels of character: the levels which we use to explain the inner workings of human actions. Behavior, we believe, is a result of motivating forces (hunger, sex, security, achievement) plus a person's ability and experiences plus an immediate physical setting. The most elementary behavior patterns are habitual. We usually think of them as being performed without conscious deliberation. Freudian psychology, however, has held even these to a closer scrutiny. In general, playwrights endow characters with speech patterns, repeated words or catch phrases, and physical tics or mannerisms in order to add comic or natural touches. When the character's attitudes toward himself or other characters enter into this, when his own awareness of that habit is stressed, when the habit results in a definite and conscious line of action in the play, then this attitudinal or habitual level is an important one indeed. Otherwise it may merely reflect a dependance on typification.

Going a step beyond attitude and habits one plumbs the level of conscious desire. What does the character really want? What are his or her goals? Contemporary actors find this to be an extremely vital link in understanding even the most minor characters in a play. Motives of this sort are not always expressed outright in the lines of a script but must be deduced often by looking back from the denouement.

When habitual behavior is thwarted a character must resort to deliberation. This exposes a whole new level of understanding. In life we do not often get to see people make these exposed choices, but when we do we have learned a great deal about them. Generally the choices are intellectual ones, but in the most profound examples of tragedy the characters are confronted with moral decisions. Assuming awareness on the part of the character of the morality inherent in this deliberation, the audience can experience the deepest possible understanding of a character in a play. A deliberation of this sort may encompass the most dramatic action of the theatre. The playwright has exposed the innermost layer of characterization when he reaches the moral level.

Form

Certain characteristics of plays allow us to categorize them according to form. Usually elements of all three forms can be found in every play, but the predominance of one or the other usually allows the audience to label what they are experiencing either as comedy or tragedy. There is also a middle form best experienced today in the "soap-opera". This mixed form, or **drame** as the French called it, usually invokes the adjective "melodramatic." Therefore we use the label melodrama for the form as well. The three forms and their features and variations can most simply be viewed in chart form (Figure 1).

FORM	TRAGEDY	COMEDY	MELODRAMA
EMOTIONS	Pity and FEAR	LAUGHTER and RIDICULE	FEAR and HATE
SUBJECT	Man's relationship to GOD or an eternal truth.	Man's relationship to his fellow man.	Life and Death Matter with TIME as a factor
THEME	Ethical Considerations	Social Situations	Pseudo-Ethical Notions
CHARACTERS	Noble Man	Ridiculous People	Evil and Virtuous
PLOT DEVELOPMENT	the Protagonist changes by an important decision	Characters Static but decide how to do something	Static Characters with Suspense as an outcome
END	to Reaffirm the dignity and nobility of Man	to Re-establish Sanity or return to Normalcy	To Reward Virtue; To Punish Evil

This chart illustrates first of all the difference in the emotions summed up in the audience during the play. Did they laugh? Did they cry? Did they boo the villan? Laughter of course is essential to comedy or at least a sense that ridiculous events are occurring. Ever since Aristotle set them out the two emotions of pity and fear have been regarded as essential to tragedy. (See next chapter 3, page 25) Pity is an empathetic emotion related to fear. We know that in this character's situation we would feel fear. Fear is the emotion we experience when someone or thing has power to do us harm, a reason to do it, and may do it soon. This emotion sounds very close to melodrama and it is, but in that type of play hatred of the ill-doer takes precedence over pity and understanding.

The subject of the play itself can be said to be inherently tragic or comic depending on factors of the conflict involved. When the central character must work out a moral dilemma, personal goals versus ethical verities, we are on tragic grounds. Comedy invariably involves inter-human relationships coupled with confusion, misunderstanding or ridiculously narrow interpretations of opposites. Melodrama is distinct here: the conflict is a matter of life and death, and time is its most important factor.

The central dilemma of a tragedy is ethical in the implications. A moral decision must be made, often between two basically moral choices whose boundaries overlap. Melodrama, since it usually hinges so heavily on time rather than choice, often presents a pseudo-serious argument whose alternatives are too obvious for consideration. Comedy of course, deals in society and its demands and conflicts.

Though most plays have a variety of characters in them, the playwright can endow them with predominately tragic, comic, or melodramatic characteristics. When character are all-good or all-evil we call them melodramatic. Any character in a play whose qualities are pushed beyond the norm become ridiculous or comic. The central character in a tragedy is harder to describe. The term most used is noble. Something sets the individual above the rest and makes him or her admirable to audiences.

Tragedy is the only form that requires a change in its characters. This change also has as a prerequisite self awareness. In comedy the character may have made a decision and in melodrama he may have survived, but both are basically the same static personality.

Children define comedy and tragedy by whether the hero dies or marries at the end. Something more basic is arrived at however. Tragedy elevates the spirits of the beholder and offers a sense of that same nobility we attributed to its central character. Comedy usually works out a balance, puts things back in order. But it often offers the definite possibility that it can all go on again since those same static characters only need a new set of circumstances. Melodrama stands out by its need to punish and reward and usually to directly state a moral.

Style

Even plays of the same type or form vary widely because of what we have come to designate as their style. Style is at its most obvious in methods of performance (scenery, costumes, acting), but even the story itself can have qualities that attribute to it a style of expression. These qualities may stem from a particular historical period, or a national concept, or more clearly originating in the vision of a particular artist, the playwright. This is true because style always uses as its basis the understanding of its audience and that audience's perception as to what is real and true. In the broadest sense there are two opposite ways of looking at the theater to begin with. First it is possible to view the play as a deliberate fake, a departure from reality. Artists call this a **stylization** and in theater terminology it is **presentational**. Others feel the theater should replicate reality whenever possible and their effects are called **representational**.

Presentational Theatre

Presentational theatre is best illustrated by the Greek actor chanting and dancing his role wearing a mask and an actor's uniform rather than street clothes. Shakespearean actors reciting long verse monologues in an elevated, ranting voice while directly acknowledging audience members on stage in chairs also come to mind. And of course there is the contemporary musical stage chorus members bursting into song and dance to express a poignant plot turn. Other presentational style marks are exposed lighting fixtures, follow spots that cause a circle of light to pinpoint central characters in a scene, the use of suggestive scenery, a clown's makeup which is a deliberate departure from reality. In effect any attempt in script or presentation of it to remind the audience that it is watching a show, a presentation. The simple device of direct address to the audience, waiting for laughs, and even the formal curtain call are presentational elements present in the most realistic stage presentation. When they are an obvious part of the play itself the play is sometimes classified as theatricalism in style.

Representational Theatre

At the opposite sensibility is the kind of theatre that tries to strengthen the illusion that everything is actually happening as the audience witnesses it. Actors do not recite or sing, but attempt to give the impression that they are real people speaking real words just as they occur. They may even turn their backs on their audiences and mumble. No costume, no makeup, no fakery at all is allowed at the extreme edge of this style. If lights are used they must always have or appear to have a natural source. The playwright's success depends on his ability to recreate what his audience accepts as real or natural. Thus he is representing reality not stylizing it. This aim gave rise to a number of realistic styles.

The isms

Within the boundaries of these two broad style categories a number of more specific and sometimes short-lived styles have developed. Given names like Neo-classicism, Romanticism, Naturalism, Expressionism, these styles have also had their reflection in the other fine arts if indeed they did not develop from them. They will be discussed at greater length in the historical chapters where they are significant. There have also been a a few entirely theatre oriented styles such as that of the **Commedia dell arte** and the **Epic Theatre**. We can say that the modern **musical theatre** has developed a specific and unique style which affect plays written for it. These styles also bear specific and more detailed analysis and so will be discussed when their presence feels its effect in the historical continuum.

Plot, theme, character, form, style are all aspects of the story. And interdependent as they are, each contributes a distinct element of the theatrical experience to an audience. It is that audience and its perception we must next analyze.

The story of **Androcles and the Lion** has tragic possibilities (Christian condemned to the beasts in the arena) and also melodramatic touches (good Greeks versus evil Romans). G.B. Shaw, however, used it as a springboard for satire and his usual dry witty dialogue. Production characteristics therefore must also follow this comic intent. Here we see a deliberately stylized forest glade colorfully unrealistic costumes (the lion is orange corduroy) and presentationally symmetrical action. Note also the humanized lion, cast and made up to pose no threat and making Androcles and his wife's terror even more comic in contrast.

Chapter Three

The Audience: What does it bring? What does it take away?

The easiest way to approach an understanding of audience is to realize that we are one. Every day man, the social animal, participates in group endeavors which shape his knowledge. Students in particular gather in various sized groups to observe an individual in the activity of teaching. Much of the knowledge they gain in this way is imparted and reinforced not only by the instructor but through the very group of which they are part. And the validity of this knowledge is checked against the values and expectancies brought to this group by each individual.

Purpose and Expectancy

This has particular applications in the theatre. Here, however, the purpose of assembling the audience is almost always regarded as entertainment. The purveyors of the theatrical event may have a far more serious goal in mind as we shall see in our historical survey but the audience nearly always attends with diversion and personal enjoyment uppermost in mind. "How did you like the play? Did you enjoy it?" Are the universal questions asked of people leaving a play. The ensuing judgment makes every audience member an amateur critic and calls upon a number of expectancies on his part. Some of these relate to the very characteristics of the play which we have already discussed.

Plot

Was the story line clear? Did it have a satisfactory beginning, middle, and end? Was it believable or possible? Did I experience empathy? In some historical periods only certain stories were allowed to be told and the audience came prepared only for these, but often knew most of the details in advance. Modern audiences tend to expect original plots.

Theme

Did the lesson agree with my own thoughts on the matter? Did I come to a new conclusion about these notions? Usually an audience dislikes being preached at and tends to choose play-going experience on the basis of other characteristics. Playwrights and producers however tend to justify their efforts on the basis of thematic content.

Character

Was there a recognizable protagonist? Did I believe those people would do and say those things? Again was there a feeling of empathy here? Could I feel myself doing those things? Often audiences are drawn to a personality and his or her story. or it may be they have come to see a particular actor or actress whose personality becomes the characters of the story in a unique way.

Form

If it was a tragedy: Did I cry? If it was a comedy: Did I laugh? The tendency to categorize the purpose of a play and then expect a certain emotional result often leads an audience astray. Nonetheless form very often is the very purpose which draws them. Each form has its entertaining characteristics for a group.

Style

Did I believe that? Was it real? Or merely a fantasy? Often it is the very style itself that becomes the purpose for the theatrical event and draws the audience to it. And it's often this style and adherence to it or departure which will serve the audience's critical judgement. Again we have to return to that word expectancy.

Conventions

Another thing every audience brings with it is a tolerance for certain conventions of the theatrical event. Many of these are purely physical: seating arrangements, curtains or lights, make-up or masks. Some pertain to the acting of the story: singing or natural delivery, men portraying women. In earlier periods audiences came expecting a prologue character to outline the plot for them. We come today expecting a printed program to identify actors. Earlier audiences expected a jolly dance and a parade sequence to end the show. Modern audiences are disappointed if the actors don't come out at the end to bow and acknowledge applause. Because they are part of the theatre to the audience these conventions must also be an important element of our study of theatre.

Aristotle and Criticism

Criticism of the theatrical event also makes use of philosophical standards which have come to serve the employ of even the most ordinary audience member. As we have seen, the Greek classical period supplied us with vocabulary still in use in the discussion and study of theater. it also supplies us with the first critical analysis of theatre, a treatise by **Aristotle** (384-22B.C.) on the **Art of Poetry** which contains our first working definition of tragedy and also contains a framework for the understanding of playmaking. Many of his conclusions, arrived at from the observation of the earliest plays we have, have nonetheless become almost common places in even a contemporary audience's belief as to what a play should be. Therefore they bear examination as a part of audience understanding and expectancy.

Tragedy defined

Aristotle's definition of comedy did not survive, but his definition of tragedy even though it has been subject to widely varying interpretation has served as a foundation for all formal and informal discussion. Tragedy, he declares, is (1) an imitation (**mimesis**) of an action that is serious, entire, and of a proper magnitude; (2) using pleasurably embellished language; (3) proceeding not by narration but by directly presented action; and (4) effecting through pity and fear a purgation (**katharsis**) of these emotions. (1)

---

(1) Translation by Philip Wheelwright. Aristotle Odyssey Press, Inc. 1935.

We have already dealt with most of these notions in our previous discussion. As we progress to the historical aspects of theatre we will return to parts of this definition to study how varying interpretations have caused scholars, theatre practitioners and audiences alike to judge the theatrical events of their era in new ways. For example the Neo-classical critics of the 18th and 19th centuries insisted on the necessity for drama to abide by what they labelled **Aristotle's Three Unities**. These so called Aristotelean principle (time, place and action) were an elaboration of the first point of the definition. Audiences of the period provoked riots on occasion of the perceived violation of these supposed rules. Expectancy in this case was shaped by philosophical tenets and their practical application to the performance. It should be noted that even in this earliest of definitions action is a necessary ingredient. Also an audience reaction or katharsis became an expectancy no matter how we translate and interpret that word.

The six parts

Another influential element of **the Poetics** was Aristotle's device of breaking the play into six parts as bases for analysis. These were: plot, character, thought, diction, music, and spectacle. We have already spent some time discussing the first three: plot or story, character, and thought or as we call it theme. Diction we covered as dialogue in our study of character.

Aristotle regarded the last two as the least important elements of the drama, probably because each is more closely related to the play in production than to its literary (Poetic) perception. Of these, music, seems to a modern audience to be only an adjunct not a necessary part of theatre. Unless attending a musical or an opera audiences tend to not even notice music unless its presence is unpleasantly obtrusive. This factor, however will also be a historical consideration. As for spectacle, the elements of costuming, scenery, lighting, in fact all physical matters of staging are usually completely the result of contemporary practices. They do, however, resoundingly have effect on the way an audience perceives the theatre and they have developed artistic skills unique to theatre with a vocabulary and discipline of their own. We will observe these as both historical developments and as contemporary phenomena in later chapters.

The well-made play

Twentieth Century audiences tend to view the play with the same scientific eyes they turn on all life around them. Everything has a purpose and an explainable source and reasonable men can find it out. A performance of a play presents to its audience a series of questions which must be answered. The process of seeking and satisfying these questions is the essence of audience involvement. This theoretical explanation of how the human mind functions has allowed the arrival at an overview of playwriting and production based on logical analysis. If nothing happens without a reason then the art form should prepare its audience so they can follow that reasoning. This careful play of preparation has come to be known as the well-made play and it is the basis or point of departure for all contemporary theatre. It also will serve us in our historical analysis as you will see.

MDQ

At the heart of every play is a state of unstable equilibrium. We have already stated the necessity for an action here and a fuse to set it off. The audience must first question the need for this action. Then they must begin to question the outcome. What will be the result of this course taken by the protagonist? When this is satisfactorily answered the audience can go home. Such an all-important question has come to be labeled the **Major Dramatic Question** of the play. That is: the central question the audience is asking itself, the answer to which satisfies them that the play is over. To state it succinctly a member of the audience must have in mind a protagonist and a clear view of his attempted action and then a final outcome.

It has already been stated that preparation is necessary to help us answer questions. Human behavior requires an understanding of motives. Natural phenomena answer to a different set of rules but must be explained nonetheless. Such preparation in a play is called **exposition**. Since a play must condense the events of a story it often begins at a point close to its inevitable conclusion. The **point of attack** or moment at which the play begins may be the moment at which the Major Dramatic Question first arises or that may come later. A play however must have near the beginning a circumstance or event that serves to start the action rolling. This we know is called the **Inciting Incident**. The **Introduction** of the play is the portion of the play between the precipitation of the action and the projection of the **Major Dramatic Question** and usually is concerned with exposition.

Many events and facts pre-dating the beginning of the play will be important to an understanding of the eventual action. This **Antecedent Action** must also be brought to the audience's attention by means of exposition. Sometimes this is performed by characters invented simply for that purpose such as the butler and feather duster yielding maid who traditionally opened French comedies of the past century. These are called **Expository** characters or scenes and are usually concealed in the introductory action.

Once the situation is laid out for the audience new elements can be added to effect the way the characters and the audience view the conflict. These are called **Complications**. They may pose a barrier to ongoing action, change its direction or merely give a new way of looking at it. When they merely involve opening our eyes to something they are called **discoveries**. They may be discoveries made by the character as to his own circumstances, by other characters as to his motives or actions, or merely by the audience through observation of theses actions and dialogue.

Complications and discoveries lead the action in a rising direction until a **crisis** is reached. This is a point at which some demand, some decision, some new direction of will must occur. It is the crest of a wave when the force of the water must come down somehow. The major crisis of the play, of course, occurs near the end at the major turning point when the major dramatic question must be answered. This answer is the **resolution** of the play. Or as we have already labelled it: the **denouement**.

In a play that has a particularly clear antagonist and protagonist, melodrama for example, the resolution grows out of a scene that has been labelled the **obligatory scene**. It is obligatory because audiences require presentation of a scene in which the good guy meets face to face with the bad guy and they have it out. Rather than a fight sequence it may be a discussion scene, but its characteristics are clear and its position near the resolution is obvious.

One other term used in play discussion and criticism is the designation **French scene**. This is a purely structural designation and refers to a unit of a play in which the same group of characters are on stage. When a new character enters or when one exits a new French scene begins. Classical plays are sometimes printed in this form, but modern plays break into scene only when the curtain or lights must designate a change of place or passage of time.

Now that we understand most of the vocabulary of criticism it is time to begin our historical survey.

Ben Jonson's Elizabethan comedy **The Alchemist** opens with this scene of conflict between the trio of scoundrels: Subtle, Face, and Doll Common. The fight over the spoils of their confidence racket serves as an expository scene, setting up all the facts an audience will need to know in the loosely strung series of plots and subplots that follow. Who they are. Where they are. Why they have come here. What they plan to do. How they mean to carry this out. They even pose a Major Dramatic Question: Will their nefarious plot succeed? Though they are not admirable protagonists, in the greedy world of this comedy of human foibles they become the only characters worth rooting for.

UNIT II

History of Western Theatrical Performance: A Reconstructed Chronology
What Can We Know about Its Development?

"Bravo! Is that
A world you've got there, hidden under your hat?"
The Lady's Not for Burning by Christopher Fry

Chapter Four
Athenian Origins

Ur-Theatre

All human beings share certain basic instincts, drives, and appetites which our competitive nature has led us to develop in surprising and complex ways. One need think only of the intricate and delicately varied methods of courtship and marriage which have grown up around the basic drive to reproduce, or the massive and technologically progressive means of warfare fed by what may merely be an appetite to compete. The theater as we know it most certainly finds roots in these instincts and the very human need to play them out and embellish and eventually to codify them.

In addition, homo sapiens is equipped with a brain which alone in the world of our experience feels the need to explain the confusion of natural phenomena amidst which it seeks survival (and believes such explanation is possible). Primitive tribes and societies make use of myth and ritual to explain and contain phenomena of a magical nature: the seasons, birth, the multiplicity of plants and animals, or of an unexplainably painful scope: death, disease, natural disasters. We see the use of these mythological tales and the ritual trappings surrounding their re-telling in theatre the world over.

Men, women, and children in all ages have loved to show off. To embellish or mutilate, costume and disguise their bodies and faces. To flex and distort, to prance and gyrate their limbs. To sing and chant, to recite or simply make noise with their voices or with instruments. Those most adept at any of these skills have always been given prominence and attention by their peers. At the same time it can be noted that the skilled story-teller was from the earliest societal beginnings a prominent individual in the group. As we have already seen from our definition, once this storyteller becomes a show-off in front of a group, theatre is born.

Lost as it is in the mists of pre-history perhaps no single event of this nature can be pointed out as the birth of theatre. All tribes, all societies found their own members and means to achieve this level. We do have, however, a series of recorded events and names on which we can be certain theater as we know it today in the Western World finds foundation. Many of our practices, methods, theories and even the content of our present-day theatre were formulated in Greece in the 5th century, B.C.

Festival Foundations: Athens

In the year 534 B.C. the city state of Athens established a contest for tragedy to be held as a part of the **City Dionysia**, a major celebration near the end of March in which the citizens rejoiced over the renewal of the crops brought by the promise of Spring. A relatively new festival, like the god it honored, **Dionysus**, whose worship had first been imported from Asia to Greece in the 13th C. B.C., the Dionysia developed rapidly to become the most popular and prestigious event in the Athenian calendar year. The mythic legend of Dionysus told of a virile and handsome young man who was slaughtered and dismembered, but after burial he miraculously resurrected in a body as perfect as before. His worship was associated with fertility and the seasonal cycles of growth; its symbols were grape vines and the thyrsus, a phallic staff associated with the Satyrs who were said to have reared him as a boy, and its rites included ecstatic revelry and wine-induced orgies, the latter being more familiar to us from his Roman name Bacchus, as bacchanalia. The City Dionysia, the largest of the four festivals in his honor, had been celebrated earlier by performances of **dithyrambs**. These choral odes or hymns were sung and danced by choruses of 50 men or boys with the aid of a choral leader who sometimes improvised a story from legend or myth. These later developed into a written form serving as the basis for the first contests. The contest for tragedy therefore signalled a further development: an individual actor had stepped out of the chorus to enact a character in the legend and address the chorus and its leader in poetic dialogue. The individual ancient Greeks credited with this innovation was also the winner of the first Athenian contest. We are all familiar with his name; it was **Thespis**. From his name we derive the word thespian.

The Greeks seemed to have loved competition of all kinds. In addition to the Olympiads, athletic contests were part of all religious festivals as were lyre playing, Homeric recitations and horse racing. But the contest for tragedy gives modern students of theatrical history a benchmark in the development of drama as we know it today. For from these religious contests in the city of Athens came the thirty-three plays which are all we have of Classic Greek Tragedy. Around

501 B.C. another innovation appeared at the Dionysia with the addition of a contest for Satyr plays. We have today the text of only one of these. Then in the year 487 or 486, a contest for Comedy was established and from these only eleven plays by one author have survived to our day. In 449 B.C. came the first contest for actors in the dramas. We have lists of the winners of these many contests, but little information of them other than the forty-odd surviving manuscripts taken from copies made by Byzantine scholars.

We owe the fact of the contests not only for our sense of a calendar of these early plays, but also what little we know of their production. The play texts do not contain staging instructions and if any early writers felt it worthy to write of such matters, this work has not survived. The illustrations of these events which we have are from paintings and cannot accurately convey performance when the designers' needs come first. The only theaters of the 5th C. B.C. have disappeared beneath Roman structures of a later period that necessarily made alterations to suit the conquerors tastes and methods. But the fact that these plays were part of a contest or religious holiday does give us something historical to tie our knowledge to.

Wherever there is a contest, there will be:

a) names of winners

b) rules of participation

Whenever religion is involved, we can expect:

a) taboos and restrictions

b) formalized ritual

And both will mandate a need to keep records. It is from such meager suppositions that most of our knowledge of the Greek theater has been forged.

First let us consider the plays themselves. Why do we have so few? How representative are those few? How did they survive and in what condition?

We do not know what a working script looked like to the Athenians of the 5th C.. B.C. We have none. What we have are copies made by the Byzantine scholars and transported to Rome when Constantinople fell to the Turks. in 1453. During the Renaissance they were translated into modern languages. it should be remembered that the Classical Greek language of the early playwrights did not survive into the modern era. Classical Latin was kept alive by the Catholic Church, but this church saw things Greek in origin as pre-Christ and therefore pagan and barbaric. Purges by the early church marked for destruction anything connected to early religious ritual and myth. In addition what few copies of the early pays that were collected into private libraries suffered. The library at Alexandria is an example. This was the acknowledged wonder of the Roman era. Here some said were collected every known book of the ancient world. One Roman scholar claimed to have read more than 800 comedies alone there, and counting the long lists of contests and winners there must have been more than 1000 tragedies as well. The library however was destroyed in a series of disastrous fires, one of which was deliberately set by Julius Caesar to create a diversion and allow his forces to regroup during his early campaign in Egypt. His tactic was successful, but our store of literary knowledge suffered irreparable loss.

Three Tragic Playwrights

What did survive as we have already learned included some 40 odd plays by 5 playwrights. Fortunately these 5 were acknowledged in their day and in later generations as the best of the lot. From **Aeschylus** the old master of Athenian tragedy, who was credited with adding a second character to the dramatic story, we have seven surviving plays. Included is the only surviving integrated trilogy: The **Oresteia**. **Sophocles**, his younger rival who added a third character actor and who seems to have been a favorite playwright in his day winning more contests than all others, has seven among the survivors. **Euripides**, somewhat of a rebel, was controversial in his own day but became increasingly popular to later generations. We have nineteen works attributed to him including the only surviving Satyr play: **The Cyclops**.

Two Comic Playwrights

Of Greek comedy playwrights until recently we only had those of the master of so-called "Old Comedy," **Aristophanes**, represented with only eleven plays. Until 1959 only fragments by the man whom the classical world regarded as the master of them all: **Menander**. In that year a complete play surfaced somewhere in the Middle East, and perhaps more are forthcoming. We also have the example of the Roman comic playwrights, among whom it was a given condition and point of pride to admit at the beginning of the play that he was merely translating a Greek masterpiece and almost always a work of Menander.

What we have, therefore, seems to represent a haphazard and yet highly personal selection out of what appears to have been the best of the Athenian contest plays. While covering a wide spectrum of dramatic possibilities they also share certain literary characteristics from which we can draw conclusions about 5th century theaters.

Characteristics of Greek Drama

1) All of the plays were written in verse and suggest some musical accompaniment.

2) All feature a chorus in scenes and also between the scenes of action.

3) All deal with a few heroic legends familiar to the Greek audience but often treated with novel and original features. Only the new comedies and one of the tragedies deal with current life.

4) All delight in an Agon or dramatic debate.

5) Another standard feature is the use of grand rhetorical solo speeches often by a messenger relating off stage events.

6) Dialogue between two characters is often in alternating complete lines of verse. That appears to be a stilted restriction but creates a driving and highly charged exchange which the Greeks called **stichomythia**.

The tragedies deal with the events leading up to or caused by a murder and sacrificial death and the working out of retribution or justice, often using the Gods themselves for convenient solutions. They make use of a point of attack late in the story and a markedly condensed time span. the comedies always hinge on a comic notion or idea (What would happen if...?), which requires a looser time frame and allows a wide span of contemporary satire. They end on a note of fertility with a festive wedding procession or **komos**. The Satyr plays burlesque the tragic legends and use a chorus of goat-like satyrs.

Literary Forms

The literary structure of the play as we already know was in verse. Paintings on vases, references in the comedies, and Aristotle's listing of the six parts all indicate this required a musical accompaniment of pipes, strings, or cymbals. The play opened with a prologue. This is a scene involving one or two characters alone on stage reciting necessary information about the background of the story. Since there were no printed programs this was provided even though the outline of the story would already be known to the audience. Still it was necessary to establish the time in the story in which the play was to take up action, to describe locale needed and to lay out certain characters featured. In the comedies it was necessary to set up the comic idea which the play would hilariously illustrate.

Then follows the **parados**. This section brings the entrance of the chorus and its leader, without which the play itself cannot begin. As the word suggest, this may have been accomplished by a formal **parade** into the **orchestra** or "dancing space" which the chorus occupied during the play. Often, however, the scripts suggest a scattered entrance from varied locations., At any rate, the parados was needed, to bring on the 12 or 15 men who made up this important feature of the scripts, so important that they usually are the title characters of the drama. Likewise, a similar feature, the **exodus**, is required at the end of each play to clear the acting area.

The body of the play is made up of a series of acted scenes between as many as 3 characters and the chorus or choral leader. These were labelled **episodes** and separated from each other by choral **odes**. The fact that these episodes were usually five in number seems to have led Renaissance scholars to declare that a classic play required five acts. This practice holds even today in the printing of classical tragedy.

Though characters in the drama could exit or enter during or after these episodes, the chorus remained present from their first entrance. The choral odes or **stasima** thus besides being an element present from the parent dithyramb contest could be used to cover time passage, carrying out of offstage business, or good old suspense and building up for horrible revelations. In comedy it sometimes suggests changing locale and thus scenic background. More importantly, at least to its audience and judges in the 5th C., it is the poet's opportunity to shine. Sometimes, therefore, the stasima are hardly related to the story at all, but seem to a modern sensibility to be mere artistic flights of fancy. Many are chauvanistic or patriotic anthems about Athens and her glories. Some feature out and out direct address to the judges to select this play for the prize. Comic choruses feature tongue twisters, animal and bird imitations and a section of great length which was to be recited in one breath. The stasima were broken into sections called **strophe** and **antistrophe**, literally a turning, and a turning against. This suggest not only the argumentative nature of these odes, but a dance movement, as well as a necessity to divide the chorus into two smaller units. Indeed the chorus serves to work out at times the problems the play's characters bring to light. At other times it serves as arbiter of the Agon or debate occuring in the episodes.

Manuscript Form

We are a little insecure about other details of the scripts because of the conditions under which they survived and the methods used to copy them. Ancient copyists used papyrus rolls to record their books. These were then rolled and stuffed into jars sealed with a skin for a lid. Walking into an ancient library must have been somewhat like walking into a modern wine cellar with its shelves lined with the bottoms of many round jars. Dry desert air preserved papyrus best, but those discovered all suffered damages. The edges would of course wear, losing key words at the ends of lines of copy. Or the outermost shell containing either the first or last scene, depending on how the scroll was rolled, might be beyond repair. To preserve space on the page these earliest manuscripts make no identification of speakers, and no staging instructions, even entrances and exits are not indicated. What we see in modern translations, then, are the result of scholarly guesswork over the ages.

Production Methods

To help us with the guess work we have some meager information on staging methods from a variety of sources. First the theatres themselves. The plays we have we know were written to be performed in the Athenian City Dionysia. The first permanent theater built there was not constructed until the year 330 B.C. This is some fifty years after the death of Aristophanes. We can therefore only assume that the stone structure on the side of the Acropolis at the shrine of Dionysus, since it is built on the site where the earlier dated plays were performed, is a permanent copy of the earlier wooden structure. Logic, of course, can be misleading. Certain things however can be determined from this and other theatres built throughout the Greek world to duplicate or outdo the Athenian original. **Virtuvius**, a Roman writing in the time of Christ, verified much of our architechtural terminology as well.

The hillside itself became the most noticeable feature ringed as it was with rows of wooden and then stone benches segmented into sections by stepped aisles from top to bottom. Labelled **Theatron** or viewing place, this audience area was selected for sight lines as well as accoustics. At the bottom ring were special seats for the judges or high priest and a small wall separating it from a large circular area where the chorus performed. This was called the **orchestra** or dancing place from the Greek word "orchesis" or dance. The center of this space contained the altar or **Thymele**. On the side opposite the theatron the orchestra was bordered by a **skene**. Since this word means hut or tent, the skene probably began simply as a shelter into which the actors could go to change masks. Later, however, it developed into a scenic front of some kind with upper stories for the Gods and scouts and five doorways for the actors to use for entrances and exits. A raised stage the length of the front of the skene became the area from which the actors addressed the chorus in the orchestra, and of course, beyond them the rising tiers of the audience. At the sides of this stage two alleyways or **paradoi** led from orchestra to the offstage area where the chorus assembled before and after each play. (See Figure 2)

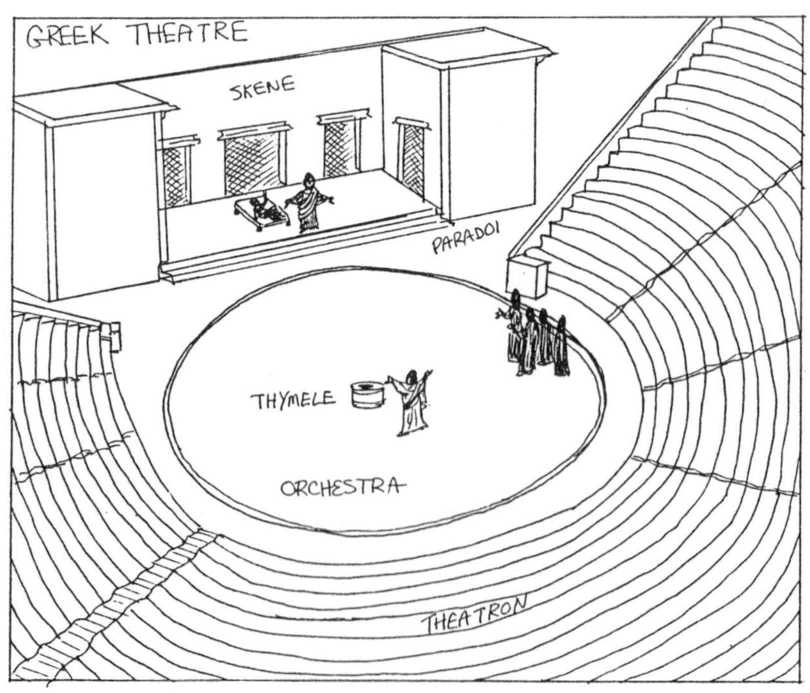

The outdoor theatre space precludes use of curtain or sophisticated lighting. Beginnings and endings of plays must be marked by a deliberate entrance and exit. And as we have seen the chorus must be given time to enter to a fixed choral ode. The permanent stage house requires an explanation in each play and the characters almost always explain why they are outside and not inside their palaces or houses. The placement of the altar in the center of the orchestra serves in may of the plays as a location for religious ritual in the story. In addition to the chorus, the principals are sometimes first seen riding in chariots or carts which would have required the paradoi to bring them into the orchestra.

Staging devices

From Vitruvius and other sources such as the comedies of Aristophanes which often poke fun at staging conventions, we know the theatres had some ingenious equipment. Foremost was the **machina**. A large crane or pulley and lever device mounted to the top of the skene, this was an extremely intrusive and noisy piece of equipment according to Aristophanes. It was used to fly Gods in and out, and since they often appeared miraculously at the end of a tragic play to straighten things out without previous preparation it has lent itself to the expression we still use for such events: **deus ex machina** or "God out of the machine" endings. A rolling platform or wagon was used to expose or bring on dead bodied or gory tableaus. This devices was required by the taboo against violent events occurring on stage. Nothing, however, prevented the showing of the results of tragic carnage for the moral edification of the throng. This rolling device was called: **ekkyklema**.

The term we have the least understanding of was something called **periaktoi**. These were scenic devices of a triangular nature mounted so that they could pivot. Perhaps different scenery was painted on each surface allowing for scenic changes, but since these were not required in the tragedies other uses have been suggested. Rapid rotation might suggest lightning or storms, or they may have been only needed between the plays of a trilogy. Some of Aristophanes comedies involve travelling scenes and the building of structures for which these could be used. Sophocles is credited with the first use of scene painting, and Euripides is chided for his shabby realistic costumes and we know from Aristotle's list of the six necessary parts that spectacle was a consideration in the contests. Albeit, the least important in his consideration.

Actors and Acting

From such sources as the lives of the playwrights and the contest rules themselves we gain insight into the acting of these dramas. Many of the stories may be apochryphal, but they serve to illuminate what is always a tenuous area of theatrical production. Like the playwrights, the Greek classical actors were ordinary citizens. Only later did this formalize itself into a profession. Furthermore, because of the religious nature of the endeavor, they were all men. Choruses said to represent women, characters of women in the tragic legends, even the female gods such as Athena were played by male performers. This does not, however, mean that the actor attempted to skillfully portray females through pose, gesture, and voice change. All evidence indicates that the mask alone indicated female characters to the audience. The actor behind the mask made no attempt to alter voice or mannerisms allowing the mask to convey the portrayal.

The **mask** was of course a required part of the actor's equipment. We are all familiar with the standard symbols of tragedy and comedy copied from mosaics, wall frescoes and statues. None of the originals have survived. They would have been made of cloth or leather molded over frames. They represented types which were readily identifiable to their audiences: young man, old miser, prostitute, hag. Some were so realistic that they terrified the women in the theatron. Socrates himself is said to have stood up during one of Aristophanes' comedies so the audience could compare his face with the amazingly realistic satirical version used by an actor. In addition to instant recognition in the large outdoor space the mask helped the actor overcome another need brought on by the rules: playing more than one role. We know that after Sophocles added a third actor the rules were frozen. No more than three principals and a chorus could be used in each play. Extras who did not speak could be used for servants, guards, soldiers, or children. When the story required additional characters (masks as the Greek manuscripts called them) it would be necessary for one of the three on stage to exit into the skene and change masks to return in a new role.

Again we must remember that the mask and perhaps some props were the only change necessary. This was a pure form of presentational acting. The choral training of the singing actor, the ritual basis of the drama, the outdoor distances to be covered dictated a stylized gesture and a formalized delivery pattern. At any time he could be required to break into full song. The chorus of course sang and danced or chanted responses in the orchestra.

Costumes seem also to have been standardized for audience recognition. As we learn from the story about Euripides' censure sited above the audience and judges did not expect to see realistic street clothing in a classic tragedy. No modern dress versions were tolerated! In comedy, along with other relaxing of rules, costumes also were different as we see on vase friezes. Comic actors wore padded suits that covered legs and arms. This allowed for exaggerated body parts, particularly the sex organs both male and female. Female characters had huge breasts and buttocks. Men had pendulous leather phalluses hanging below comically too-short skirts. These allowed for much scatological and outright bawdy physical humor in the plays which is only hinted at in the lines as often prudishly translated today. Not even the gods were excepted from this satirical view. Hercules, the quintessential "dumb jock" of the classical world would be readily recognized by his lion skin and the bulging muscles of his padding. The new comedy of Menander as it moved into more contemporary domestic situations required costumes and masks to suit the trend.

Let us consider what we know of the contests themselves. Citizens of Athens who wished to have their plays performed were required to "apply for a chorus" to the Archon or chief magistrate a year in advance. Three tragic poets and five comic ones would be chosen, and each assigned a well-to-do citizen to act as a sponsor. This citizen, called a **choregos**, took no part in the performance but oversaw and helped pay for hiring and rehearsing and costuming the performance in the year before its presentation. Of course it was an honor if his production won, but there were no cash prizes. Each tragic poet was to present three tragedies and a Satyr play. He was expected to prepare a chorus and choral leader, three actors, and the necessary extras and of course had a year for rehearsal and necessary rewrites, adjustment of music, preparation of dances. None of these people, it must be remembered, were full-time professionals. The great numbers of personnel needed including the dithyramb choristers and the five comedy casts must have made up a uniquely understanding and critical audience. We have no record of any individual man who acted in both comedy and tragedy. Nor of anyone who wrote both types.

Audiences

The audience for the performances consisted of all of the Athenian citizens. Those who could not pay the minimal admission were admitted free. Prisoners were released to be able to attend. It was also a matter of pride to let foreign visitors attend. They would have been subjected already to days of ceremonies for Dionysus. Dithyramb contests with their large participation came first. Then a day set aside for the comedies. Then three days for tragedy, one for each playwright. Of course the audience was prepared to sit in the open on the stepped off hillside. They had come to enjoy and critique men from their neighborhood singing the story while they posed and danced in ritualized costumes and masks. Although the events of the story would have been familiar to them they expected a prologue to set forth the background needed followed by a series of episodes which set forth thrillingly events of the tale, often improvising new and surprising plot turns. These would be interspersed with choral passages. A good moral debate, a harrowing messenger narrative, some clever character analysis and soul-searching word play, an appropriate appearance by a god or goddess were to be anticipated. and of course if it was comedy day lots of bawdy horseplay and gossipy social satire on contemporary people in the audience or well known to it. Even the tragic performance always ended with the short satirical take off on a serious story line.

Reading a Greek Play

In reading the plays today we need to remember the following:

The Chorus

1) Perhaps the most foreign element to a modern audience, the chorus was essential to dramatic structure.

2) It almost always expresses the audience's doubts, reasoning and eventual decision.

3) It functions in an episode usually only as a listener, but it is always there.

4) The choral odes are often merely beautiful verse and can be studied as such.

The Characters

1) Some seem to be merely sketched in because the Greek audience already knew details of their lives and character.

2) No modern psychological inner dialogue works here; characters say what they mean and why they act the way they do, even when the chorus can overhear them.

3) In comedy the characters' names are usually punned or based on contemporary Athenians so they don't have the comic ring to our ear that they would have to their audience.

4) You will need in your mind's eye to supply most of the action and spectacle.

The Language

1) Translators usually apend a note explaining their approach to the versification. Read it!

2) Most contemporary references in the comedies are explained in modern terminology.

3) Gods and goddesses' functions in the plays often requires a brief survey of their mythology.

4) Watch for the pithy little "bumper sticker" type wise sayings with which the poet sprinkles the play. Greek audiences loved and treasured these and quoted them years later.

The Conventions

1) Remember that Aristotle regarded plot foremost of the six parts. Each episode was chosen thus to forward this. Be sure you understand each.

2) The agon or debate is usually carefully chosen and placed to convince not only the chorus or characters in an episode, but the audience (reader) as well.

3) Don't let the choral odes distract you from the plot line.

4) Greek morality was hardly different from our own. Even the gods are subjected to a moral standard that we can still understand.

If you let the play speak to you in this way, you should understand why many regard these as not only the foundation of our Western theatrical tradition, but also the greatest examples of it.

In some modern productions the playwright handles crowd scenes like a Greek chorus. Here in Ibsen's great romantic verse tragedy **Brand** we see the agon or obligatory debate between the Archbishop and his conservative forces stage right and the uncompromising young firebrand stage left. In the Greek manner the crowd serves as an audience advocate, here obviously being swayed to follow the playwright's young protagonist. Note use of neutral, unspecific stage space. The crowd like a Greek chorus comes up out of the audience area not entirely on stage with the principal actors.

Chapter Five

The Roman Era

Commercial Cornerstones: Rome

Rome was a skillful and unabashed borrower. Like the modern English language, Roman civilization's greatest attribute was its ability to absorb and make use of the best elements of every conquered tribe, city or state. One thing they almost immediately took to heart was Greek theatre. Stone theatrons were constructed by conquering Romans throughout the known world. If a sufficient hillside was not available they constructed one of stone as they did the Colosseum in the heart of their capital. Plays "translated" from the Greek were performed in them, and the Roman playwrights outdid each other to claim the Athenians, especially Menander, as their sources. Originality was not a virtue in the Roman theatre.

Romans had enjoyed primitive forms of drama which continued to be performed after the introduction of the Greek comedies and tragedies. The **Attelan farces** were largely unscripted or in native tongues and bore simple farcical plots based on the same group of stock characters. The other prominent form consisted of mimed dance myths performed to music, which were called **pantomime**. Then, of course, the most popular form of entertainment was the gladiatoral, chariot, and battle-oriented contests of the arena. To these popular forms the Greek style drama posed competition.

Plays were performed along with these other entertainments at public holidays called in the Latin: **Ludi**. These holidays, unlike the Greek festivals, did not necessarily have a religious connotation. They were normal bi-monthly events in the Roman calendar to make up for spare days in the month. In addition, they could be called by the Senate or any wealthy citizen to celebrate a personal or public "triumph". Our modern term "bread and circuses" comes from the practice of Roman politicians who bought votes from the masses by throwing these extravagent free for all holidays. At these events the public was treated to theatre, races, fights, and free food all at once. The plays had to entertain a public that could at anytime walk next door to the Colosseum. Because of this difference in the Ludi and the Dionysian Festival we see many changes in form and performance. These changes have profoundly effected our modern practice because it is from the Romans and not the Greeks that

Renaissance practices arose. And Roman theatre was predominately a commercial venture, not a religious contest.

First, then, let us look at the plays themselves. Like the Greeks before them we have only a handful. But these come to us in a more complete and verifiable form. Since they had been written in Latin, a language that has really never died, they are more accessible to translation. The church had retained many of the comedies of the two comic writers, Plautus and Terence, and taught them regularly as examples of perfect classical rhetoric. Though probably not acted out, the scripts, particularly those of Terence, were recited and studied continuously from the Roman era until interest in production arrived in the Renaissance. We have thus twenty-one surviving plays by Plautus. All six of Terence's comedies have survived because of the high regard for his language. Nine tragedies survive, all attributed to Seneca, and though many doubt they were ever meant for production they have since the Renaissance had a deep and lasting influence.

Literary Form

Like their avowed Greek models the Roman plays are in verse. A wide variety of poetic forms are used. Sections labelled "**cantica**" or "songs" appear like operatic arias to have been sung since a musical accompaniment was always present. They may however have required only a chant or sing-song delivery. At any rate the chorus is now absent except for literary presence in the tragedies to divide the five episodes. The comedies are also divided, into episodes separated only by entrances and exits of characters. The plays feature a **prologue** usually by a nameless character who sets forth the plot and describes the setup required. In Terence's plays this **Prologus** also assumes the Greek Chorus's role of arguing with the audience and stating the worth of the author's writing. Of course, no contest award is expected, but the playwright feels it necessary when a Roman audience had so many other choices of diversion at hand. The play then progresses in rapid succession, each episode planned to hook and hold a fickle and not too discerning public. The plays are little more than an hour in length.

In addition to the verse and song forms, word play, puns and figures of **speech** are used abundantly by the playwrights. The tragedy writer particularly delights in **Sententia** or quotable maxims which often are taken from historic sources his audience would have recognized. Insult jokes are popular, as are sexual, often homosexual innuendo and very often what appear as jokes are inserted in the story without context merely to amuse the audience. Unlike the Greeks, however, topical reference and satire on local events is noticeably absent. The comedies all use Greek names and locales, but the characters are decidedly Roman in behavior and outlook. Following Menanader's pattern the plots are almost all based on family matters like our modern sit-coms: father-son quarrels, husband-wife mismatches; or like the modern soap opera: long lost children recovered, mistresses and their greed, servants and their plotting.

Tragedies continued to mine the same load of myths and stories of the Trojan War, or the house of Thebes. But what a change! No longer bound by the religious taboos of the Greek predecessors and vying as they were for a blood-thirsty audience, the plays now illustrated on stage what the Greeks could merely report by messenger. Since masks were still used it was a simple matter to substitute at the crucial moments a drugged slave or prisoner to be beheaded or disemboweled at the climax of the story. Audiences accustomed to the horrors of the arena next door could hardly expect less than the real thing in the theatre. In addition to this exaggerated and explicit sensationalism, the tragedies abound in inflated rhetorically elaborate monologues using every showy debate technique and much flowery word play. The chorus is used only as a literary device and seldom figures in the plot. Where the Greek plays had always concerned themselves with a moral debate the Roman playwright concerns himself merely with analyzing a single human perversion; revenge, guilt, lust, etc.

Two other features of these plays seem to grow out of the manner in which they had to be staged. The comedies use the device of the "running servant" and the onstage character who spies on another scene without being detected. Often two speak without others seemingly to overhear. These of course require a large or long open stage with many nooks or hiding spaces. The Roman theatre of course supplied just that. Also every play ends with one character, begging the audience for its applause. This seems to be the result of the need to inform the spectators that the plot was completed. After all the the theatres had no lights to dim, no curtain to draw or drop as we shall we see.

We shall return to much of this when we discuss Shakespeare and his contemporaries. For it must be remembered that Plautus, Terence, and Seneca were memorized by every Elizabethan schoolboy in his Latin classes.

Production Method

Wherever they found them in the colonies they conquered, the Romans rebuilt the Greek theatres setting them in stone to the new requirements of Roman drama. It is these buildings that we see today throughout the Mediterranean basin. The first permanent theatre building in Rome was constructed by Pompey in 55 B.C. This was a self-contained stone building some three or more stories in height. A semi-circular orchestra space in the center, no longer needed for a dancing chorus was used for reserved seating. Surrounded on one side by the half-circle curve of rising stone tiers for seating, it could also be covered by linen awnings but was otherwise still open-air in nature. The stage was a long raised platform longer than the circle diameter it bisected. This stage was backed by a 3-story facade or **scenae frons** of hugely ornamental nature. It contained 5 doorways, many columns and niches for statues. The upper levels also were practical for stage use, with windows and travel cat walks. The stage was roofed over which allowed for the hanging of a curtain which could be dropped into the floor at the start of the play, but could not, of course, be raised again because such roping would be seen all during the performance. (See Figure 3).

The plays themselves still require a prologue to identify the inhabitants of the doors of the permanent scenae frons. But a frequent feature of the plays is a character on stage announcing: "I hear a door opening; someone must be coming out." The exits stage left and right seems to have had a permanent connotation to the Roman audiences. One was always identified as the street to the market; the other as a road to the seaport or a foreign country.

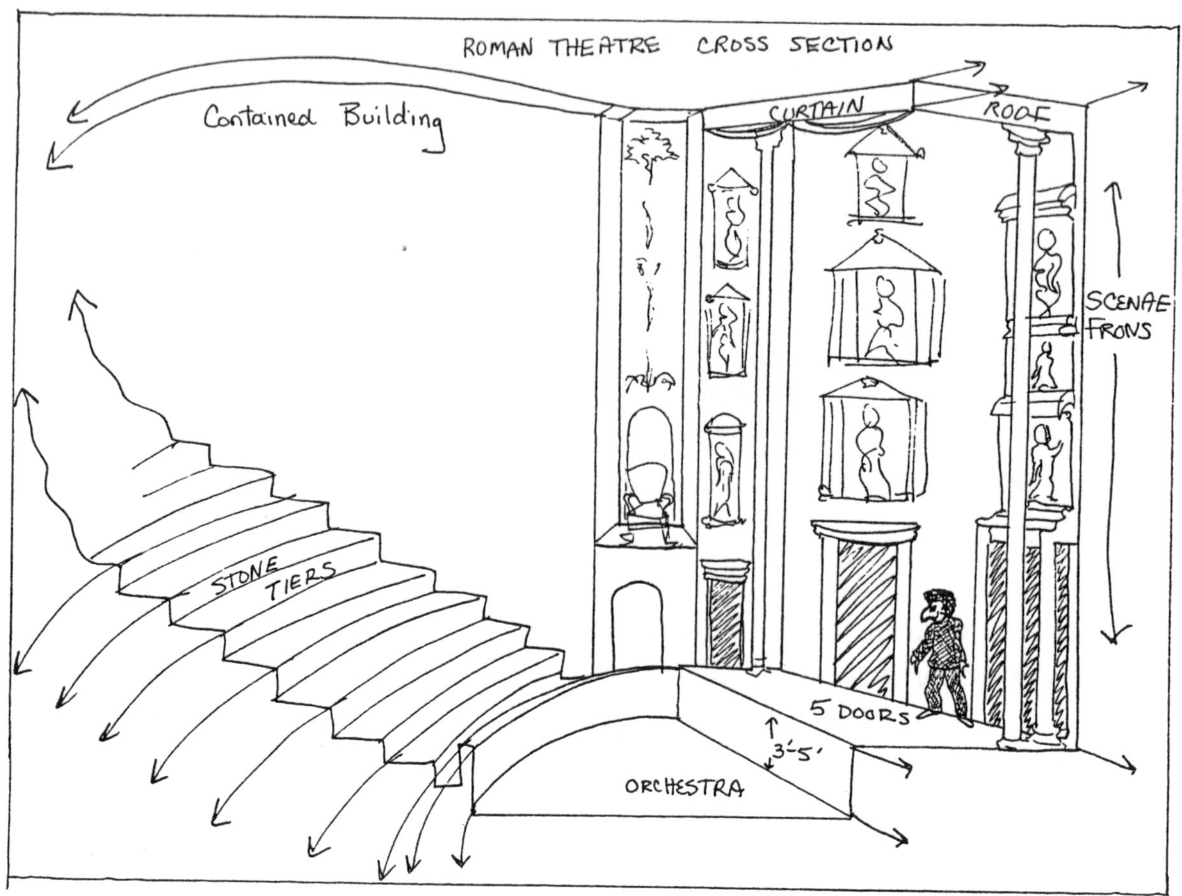

Actors and Acting

The plays themselves were performed by professionals. And as in Greece they were all men. Often slaves, they banded together like Gladiators and were highly trained. Though they did not have to dance or chant in chorus as the Greek forerunners had, they still needed to be able to sing, declaim vigorously, and master poses that represented specific emotions. The long raised stage and the rambunctious nature of the comic scripts required skilled gymnasts and breath control for the long running sprints and horse-play interspersed with the sung or spoken dialogue. Masks were used and color-coded costumes were required: red for slaves and yellow for prostitutes are two combinations we know of.

One exception to the males only rule was in the pantomime performances, where women seem to have excelled. The most famous of these performers was the empress Theodora herself who had been an "actress" before marrying the emperor Justinian. Her act consisted of lying naked on stage with strategic parts of her body covered with bird seed. Doves were released to peck at these, gradually revealing her nude form, no doubt writhing seductively to music. A clever form of striptease, this! And an indication of the reasons the church grew to dislike all theatrical performances and personnel. Justinean had to pass a law to allow himself to marry an actress, and then only on condition that any such individual swear off any future performing.

The most famous Roman actor was named **Roscius** and he like Thespis has given his named to history. The great actor of every age is referred to by his name. Burbage was the Elizabethan Roscius. Booth and many others were referred to as the American Roscius. And in our own day Olivier was often called the 20th Century Roscius.

Along with the playwrights, some actors became celebrated and honored Roman citizens. Plautus had been an actor before he was freed and became a much honored and copied poet. Terence, who seems to have been a black slave from Africa, gained such respect for his refined use of the Latin and the delicacy of emotion which he added to the standard farcical plots that he was freed and granted permission by edict of the Senate to wear the toga of nobility. So theatre, though a profession now, was not looked down on as was to be the case when Rome converted to Christianity.

As I have already stated, little is known of the writer of the tragedies although they are credited to the philosopher Seneca by their Renaissance discoverers. "Senecan" has thus become a word used in theatre to describe gratuitous horror or sadistic plays of revenge and carnage.

Reading a Roman Comedy or Tragedy

The Plot

1) The characters' names may be Greek but they invariably behave like Romans, according to Roman law and custom.
2) Time and logical behavior have no place in this farcical world.
3) The father is absolute law in the Roman household.
4) The kidnapped or stolen child is a standard element.

The Characters

1) Stock characteristics in costuming as well as behavior were conventions of the drama.

2) Where characters are given names they almost always have a comic meaning.

3) Servants are always smarter than their masters and mistresses.

4) Again remember to supply broad farcical action whenever it is hinted at in the lines.

The Language

1) Long rhetorical speeches can be thought of as songs or dramatic monologues in contemporary drama.

2) Watch for the **Sententiae**.

3) Be prepared for sexual innuendo in comedy.

4) Be prepared for gory details in the tragedies.

The Conventions

1) Think of the modern musical comedy format. (Plautus has served as model and inspiration from Moliere and Shakespeare to Rogers and Hart or Sondheim and Gelbhart.)

2) Entrance and exits cues are in the dialogue.

3) Important plot points are repeated often enough for a distracted or slow audience to absorb.

4) Don't analyze the morality of these commercially engendered plays.

The only moral code present in the characters seems to be: Everyone for himself. Think of them as pure entertainment and you will see why especially the Plautine farces are still performed to delighted audiences.

A Recognition scene was a standard element of both Greek and Roman comedy. Here the long separated title characters from Plautus' The Twin Menaechmi have to have the truth beaten home. Use of half masks and stylized wigs in the Roman manner make casting modern actors easier, but require exaggerated posture and lower face manipulation to gain comic point. Note also the obvious stock characters: crotchety old man, shrewish wife, and that purely Roman type, the parasite whose name appropriately is Sponge.

Chapter Six
Medieval Theatre

Ritualistic Shaping: The Dark Ages

The Dark Ages for theatre began not with the fall of the Roman Empire but with its conversion to Christianity in the 4th Century. The church had always been mistrustful, even outright antagonistic toward theatre not without reason: The comedies had held church figures up to ridicule; the mimes and pantomimes were often openly pornographic; and the gladitorial and animal fights had Christian victims too often. Now with the power of the state behind them, church leaders cracked down. Theatres, hippodromes, even the Colosseum were taken over for religious functions. Gladiators were abolished in 404 A.D. even though the public at large still clamored for them. Actors, classed with jugglers and other public entertainers faced excommunication and took their skills to the road. It was a long haul till the breaking light of the Renaissance began slow recognition again. They were not in total darkness, however.

The middle ages proved to be a time of tumultuous performance development. The common peasants had their roving troupes of entertainers travelling from fair to fair. The nobility in their castles and manors jealously nurtured their individual jesters, jugglers and musicians. Among Northern tribes storytelling minstrels or scops were the pride of each war lord. And even though a veritable flood of edicts issued from the authoritarian church in Rome and Constantinople, the monks and nuns of the cloistered life continued to copy and treasure the Greek and Roman dramatic literature that survived each purge. A Saxon nun by the name of **Hroswitha** even wrote a few original farces and romances on the models of Terence. Though we have not discovered others like her, she was probably not an isolated case. The Papal anathema against theatrical performances and performers during the long medieval period can only suggest a continuing and fertile stage in dramatic developments. Sadly it also explains why so little has survived from this and earlier periods.

Ironically, then, it is to the church itself that we look for a new birth of dramatic form. As Greek theatre had emerged from Dionysic ritual and stories of the Trojan war, Medieval theatre came forth from the ritual of the Mass and stories of the Christian Bible. Sometime around the year 925, the following scene and dialogue were performed in a church in central Europe. Down the center aisle of the church on Easter Sunday three young choir boys dressed in women's robes and bearing small bundles approached the altar which, traditionally representing Christ's tomb, had been draped in black on Good Friday. There they were met by a man in splendid priestly robes. He was winged and had a halo, for he represented the angel of the Lord. Raising his hand he spoke in Latin the lines that have given their name to the playlet:

Angel: Quem Quaeritus? (Whom seekest thou?)

The three Marys (for this is whom the boys were portraying) reply that they have come to embalm the body of their Lord with rare spices which they carry. Whereupon the Angel informs them that Chist is no longer there: He is risen. Then he instructs them to go forth and announce the glad tidings. Turning to the congregation they proclaim: "Alleluia."

QQ Trope

Antiphonal reading by Priest and congregation called **Tropes** were not uncommon in the Mass. But the staging of this Easter scene in what became known as the **Quem Quaeritus Trope** set another milestone in theatrical history. Out of it developed a rich liturgical drama whose popularity eventually necessitated its own expulsion from the Mother Church.

Church fathers were quick to recognize the value of staging Biblical events for their congregations. After all there were no books readily available, those few were in Latin, a language no longer familiar to the masses; and the church depended on spreading its message for its continued existence. Theatrical performances of the Easter story, the Christmas events, even the miracles of the saints could be acted out by the young clergy. Because they were no longer in Latin, but in the audiences's own language, they soon grew in popularity until the performances had to be moved outside the churches. Eventually they became so elaborate that the church turned production of them over to private and civic groups.

The Three M's

These plays have traditionally been classified as **Mystery** plays: events from Christ's life, **Miracle** plays; stories of the Saints and the Old Testament, and **Morality** Plays: allegorical tellings of Christian truths. The full telling of Christ's life, teachings, death, and resurrection, which often took a week to perform was a **Passion Play**. In England the Biblical stories were told in separate playlets but performed as part of one long festival. These were labelled **Cycle plays** and are known today not by their anonymous authors but by the City in which they were performed, such as: The York Cycle.

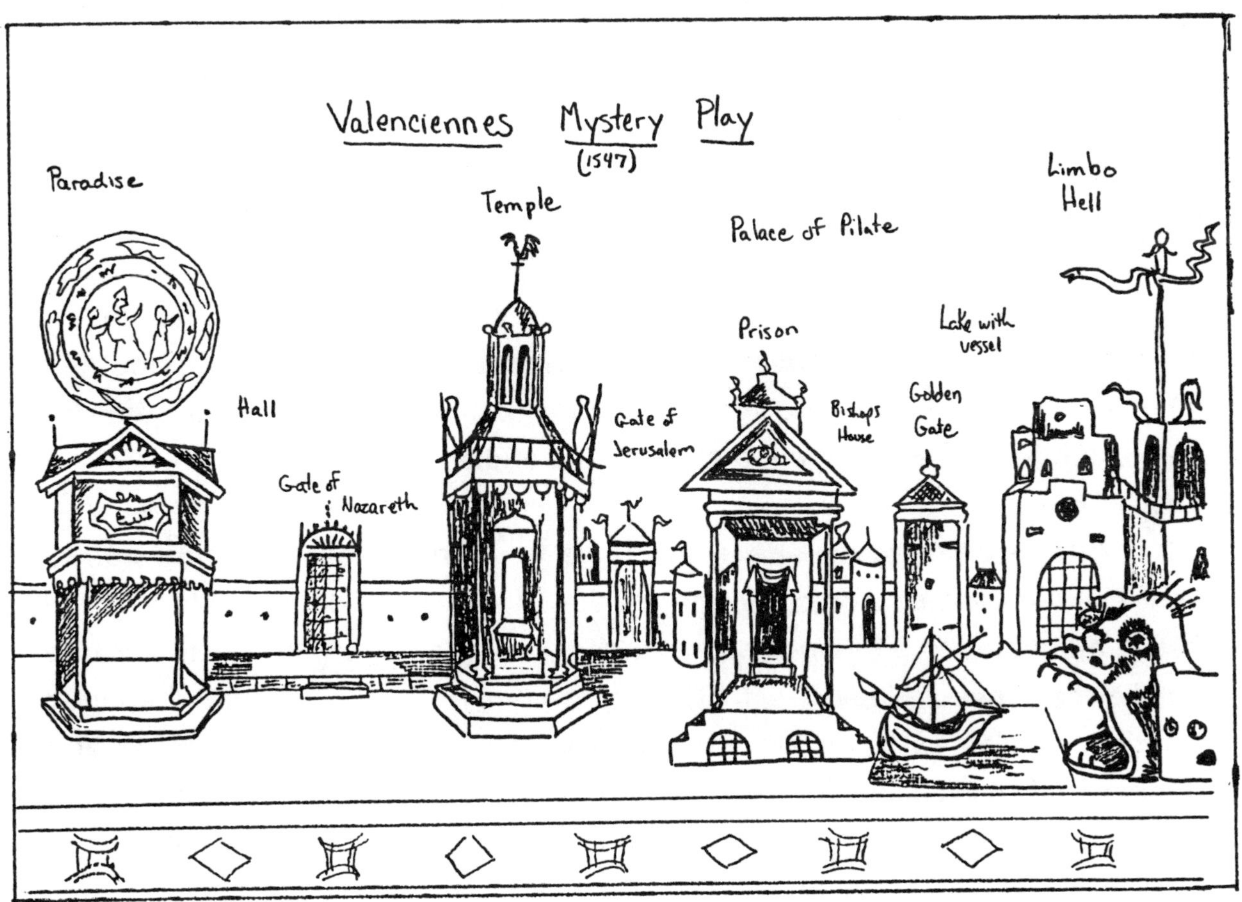

Production Methods

The interior of the cathedrals of the Middle Ages lent itself without alteration to moveable staging. Since there were no pews the congregated audience could follow the young acolytes from niche to niche along the walls of the church where stations of the cross and shrines to individual saints stood ready to serve as background. In the open center of the cruciform structure, the altar served for climactic scenes: the manger, the last supper, the tomb. When moved outside to accommodate the growing crowds, the square in front of the cathedral with its great porch needed little alteration. When the trade guilds assumed production and elaborate scenic backgrounds became practice the same staging was used. Called **mansion staging**, it consisted of a series of locations permanently before the audience around the square or along a hillside for the passion plays with a flat acting area, or **Platea**, in front which could serve in all scenes. In England where there were no great central squares, but small one scattered about the towns, each mansion was mounted on a wagon and served for each single unit play of the cycle. After each unit the cycle play would move its **wagon stage** to the next square and a new wagon would move in to present the next playlet.

An ever present feature of the mansion stages was the Hell mouth. A huge animal head in illustrations of the period it could belch forth flame and smoke. Out of it issued horrible realistic devils and gargoyle creatures who could race around and torment and terrify the audience.

It is important to remember that since the purpose of the drama was to convince the congregation of the truth of the **Bible**, every detail of staging and acting attempted to be as realistic and convincing as possible. Hell required smoke machines. Heaven with God seated in Pope-like splendor required rotating candles for stars and invisible wire and pulleys to fly cherubs and angels from the ceiling of the church and later of a mansion built for the purpose. Costuming was elaborate and specific. Records state the cost of sewing white kid skin suits for Adam and Eve who must of course appear naked.

Actors and Acting

At first of course the performers were the clergy and boys of the choir. When the plays moved outside and became civic responsibility the church taboo on women participating continued. But realism demanded that the Marys and young women be performed by attractive young boys, their voices unchanged and their demeanor in every way convincingly feminine. No vestige remained now of the Greek presentational female, whose costume alone designated the role. Boys were trained to portray women and girls as realistically as possible. Older women, such as Noah's wife who was traditionally a nagging shrew, were portrayed by older men. Comic elements of the Biblical stories were developed whenever possible: Shepherds became griping clowns, the spice salesman was a foxy con-artist, and Noah a tipsy drunkard. In addition to the scary devils, Herod and his mad "raging in the streets" was a prime serious acting part.

Staging the Passion Play

Although we do not know the authors of these scripts, many versions have survived. As have illustrations of productions and in some cases first hand accounts. The Passion plays have even continued in production, with continuous revision and re-translation, down to the present day. In Oberammergau, Germany, a presentation is mounted every ten years. In Spearfish, South Dakota, a company of German immigrants fleeing Hitler's suppression in the early thirties continued their traditional parts passing them on to their children in the summer long Black Hills Passion Play. This version shortened to allow an audience to experience it all in one evening begins with Christ's entry into Jerusalem and follows the events through the crucifixion to a final triumphant Ascension scene. Like the Medieval performance, it is cast with professional actors trained for the central roles. Townspeople amateurs fill up the crowd scenes. Real animals are used. The stage is a long platea backed with a series of mansions that are framed only by the Gates of Jerusalem on one end and the hill of Golgotha on the other. Lines of dialogue are spoken directly from the King James version of the **New Testament** and familiar religious music accompanies all scenes which often consist of dramatic and picturesque tableaus. One such is the familiar Lord's Supper painted by DaVinci duplicated by live actors while Handel's "See the Conquering Hero Comes" is played in accompaniment. In the background, over the stage, the audience on its sloping hillside open to the sky can see the electric lights of the modern city below.

Anachronism

Anachronistic? Yes! And this, too, was a feature of the Medieval drama. Medieval man did not have the view of history that modern man carries with him. All time existed in the mind of God, they felt. Therefore, all events are timeless in context. Shepherds in the Cycle plays swear oaths by "Christ's Cross" even as they kneel by the manger. Herod's troops carry muskets in illustrations and costumes are elaborate and colorful, never accurate to time and place, but contemporary to the production.

Less is known, of course, about the secular drama because of its suppression. One short farce in vernacular about a shyster lawyer called "Pierre Pathelin" has come down to us. The other popular form of the age was an improvised drama which we will discuss in a chapter all its own.

Reading a Medieval Play

The Plot

1) Standard Biblical stories still familiar to any Sunday School child.
2) Usually they are tied to a holiday or sacrament.
3) Look for obvious preaching of morality.
4) Look for a moral ending even in the comic skits.

The Characters and Language

1) Since the audience knew the parables little characterization was put in the text.
2) Quotations are directly from scripture.
3) The only verses would be hymns, otherwise the characters speak prose; at times it is very plain, then without notice becomes flowery and liturgical.
4) In the Morality plays character represent abstract ideas: friendship, lust, sloth, etc. They behave like humans, but have only one facet to their characters.

Conventions

1) Remember that with the Mansion stage the end (Tomb and Cross) is always in the audience view.
2) Don't be thrown off by the anachronisms; they are not an indication of naivete.
3) Expect to be preached at often.
4) The moral lesson will be hammered home at the end.

Attending performances of the Passion plays with an audience of families, children, and adult can be an extremely moving experience. The cycle plays, too, have recently been staged and prove to be a wonderfully varied and thought-provoking entertainment.

A modern play which requires a medieval mansion stage set is Tennessee William's **Summer and Smoke.** On stage at all times are the parlor of the parsonage where Alma teaches piano lessons and assembles her poetry reading group stage right contrasted with the doctor's office with its grossly realistic anatomy charts where young Doctor Johnny participates in a drunken party stage left. Each of these characters undergoes a passion play like series of scenes leading to a conversion and reversal during the long plague ridden summer of the play. In the center stage at all times is the park with its angel of Eternity hovering overhead and serving as the locale for the important pivotal and climactic scene.

Chapter Seven

Commedia dell'Arte

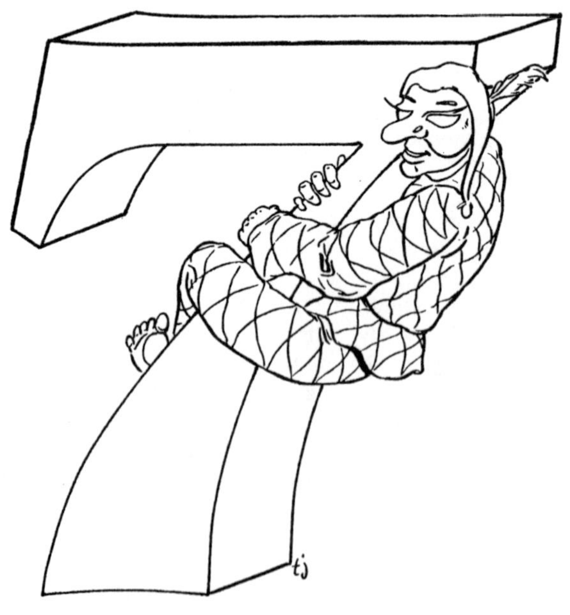

Immortal Improvisations

The Commedia is a style of performance that seems to belong to no particular era and yet to them all. Seeming as it did to have its roots in the Attelan farces, it may have sprung as well from Plautine professionals cast adrift by Rome's conversion. At any rate we see travelling performance troupes springing up in the Medieval period, a yeasty spreading growth of the style throughout Europe during the Renaissance, full flowering in the countryside and courts of the sixteenth and seventeenth centuries where its influences spread to literary forms that are still with us. From fabric design to the toy industry, from book jackets to movie screens the character names and types established by the Commedia dell'arte are with us every day. In their very unique timelessness they rate a chapter of their own.

Commedia dell'arte (comedy of professional artisans) was also called **Commedia all'improviso** because it was improvised by the artist. Performers were members of a small travelling group or troupe usually interrrelated as a family by whose name they were identified i.e., the Gelosi troupe. Originating in Italy, these small troupes travelled from town to town carrying props, costumes, musical instruments with them on small gypsy-type wagons from which they performed wherever they could rouse up an audience willing to pay. Because the plays were improvised, the actors of the troupe could perform also in town halls, courtyards, in fact any space could be utilized for their stage.

In lieu of a script the **impresario** or leader of the group merely posted a **scenario** or list of scenes in the story to be acted out. Members of the troupe knew their own roles and merely added typical dialogue and business as the performance ensued. Standard comic action or dialogue bits were called **Lazzi**, and each troupe and player had their own. Some of these have come down to us merely by name, such as: the tooth lazzi, the enema lazzi; but most would seem to still survive in circus clowning and burlesque gags.

In addition to this standard and often rehearsed stage business the troupe had another sure-fire performance device that added to the universality of their appeal. Each troupe utilized the same pool of character types common as to name, costume, and comic traits. Whether it was the Gelimaldi troupe touring Italy's boot, the Spontinis in northern Germany, or even the troupe of performers Catherine da Medici took with her to France when she married Henri II, each shared the same characters. This is another feature of the plays that made them immediately understandable no matter what language the audience spoke. These stock characters were divided into three categories: the professionals, the servants, the lovers. (See Figure 5).

The Professionals are older members of the troupe and chief among them is **Pantalone**. He is Venetian as one can tell by his accent and the slippers with curled up toes. His name comes from or lends itself to the knee britches or Pantalons that he wears. His suit and cape are red and black and he wears a black skull cap. Like the other characters of the Commedia (except for a few exceptions which I will point out) he wears a half mask of molded leather. His mask is characterized by a large hooked nose and scraggly beard. He usually carries a tall staff or cane to exert authority and use as a weapon. Pantalone's function in the plays is to thwart the lovers. He is either a parent or guardian of one or both and usually letchs after any young girl in the story. He is also a tightwad and a miser.

His friend and confidant is the Doctor or **Dottore**. Not a medicinal doctor, this one is a Doctor of Philosophy and comes from Bologna. Evidently the ancient world acknowledged the stereotype of fellows from this particular university as being "full of baloney," because Dottore is always shown as a verbose blowhard who used big words but did not understand their meaning. His costume is of course an academic gown and soft mortar board hat and tassle. His mask also sports a long, bulbous, phallic nose. And of course he also is an avid skirt-chaser.

The other senior member of the troupe was **Capitano**, the direct descendent of Plautus's Braggart Warrior. He wears a flamboyant uniform in any of the local military colors the troupe might encounter. Like the Keystone Cops of our movies, this uniform and weaponry are comically exaggerated. He is a loud, blustery braggart always telling of his conquests, but he shrinks back on the sight of a mouse and runs away from the challenge of a duel. He's usually bargaining for the young girl and his mask has a great Roman nose and fine moustaches to twirl.

Between these senior characters and the young lovers was the wonderfully varied class of servants: much put upon, often cudgeled and beaten, but ever scheming and actively manipulating the plot contrivances of their less clever masters and mistresses. They are also called as a class by their Italian label: **Zanni**. And this label has given us our modern descriptive term: zany, for that is what their actors often seem.

Foremost among the Zanni is that paragon of loveable scoundrels: **Harlequin** or in the original Italian: **Arlecchino**. His patchwork costume became so recognizable that those diamond patterns are still labelled "Harlequin patches." He always wore a black mask, probably in recognition of the cleverness and agility of African servants. He is both an arcrobat and a schemer usually used in the plot to help the young lovers overcome the old men's lecherous plans. He is a contrast of personality traits: both cleverer than any one else on stage, but sometimes naively led astray by enthusiasm for a wild idea. Always at his side is his trusty weapon, a split stick that makes a loud bang when struck against an exposed buttock or head. This is called a slapstick and gives its name to the style of comedy still indulged in by circus clowns and television sitcoms of the more physical variety.

Next to Harlequin is the wicked schemer **Brighella**. His colors are green and yellow, and he often carries a dagger because his schemes are usually to no one's good but himself. The stupid, loutish servant with a huge white shirt and clown cap and neck ruff was **Pulcinello**, who became Punch of the Punch and Judy shows still popular in England. A source of humor for his audiences was his ugly mask and the deforming humpback with which he was always portrayed. It is important to remember that physical deformity or speech impediments were sources of hilarity to these audiences.

A Zanni of an entirely different and endearing nature was **Pierrot**. With his black skull cap, floppy, white pajama-like costume, neck ruff and pompom buttons, his figure is familiar from dolls and figurines. He was unique in the Commedia in several ways. First he was the only completely mute character in the troupe. Like his modern counterpart Harpo Marx, he never spoke a word. Because the face is so important in pantomine he never wore a mask like the other characters who were verbal. Instead he painted his face clown white. His character was gentle and often love-lorn.

Of course, all of these Zanni and the professionals too could have female counterparts. Arlecchina, Pulcinella, Pierrette could be maids, confidants of the young ladies, innkeepers, or chaperones. And here it is worth noting that in these troupes women played women's roles. Their skill, attractiveness, and the spreading fame of the troupes were instrumental in breaking down the anathema against female actors.

Particularly popular were the young ladies of the **Inamorata** or the **Lovers**. Like their male counterparts these were attractive, young, and musically talented. They were expected to wear the latest fashions attractively.

Audiences in each new town expected to see what was new from Rome or Venice and also to pick up bits of gossip dropped in the dialogue from wherever the troupe had last performed. Lovers must also be able to sing and dance. They usually used their own names and did not wear masks. As they grew older, they assumed the character roles of Zanni or professionals and younger family members stepped into the lovers parts.

With these standard characterizations, the ease of staging needs, and the scriptless nature of story telling that easily crossed any language barrier, Commedia spread from Italy to every part of the continent and established itself as a universally popular theatrical form. Even though its popularity waned after the seventeenth century, its characteristic theatrical devices had become so ingrained as to continue to influence playwriting and performance methods to the present day.

Recognizing Conventions of Commedia

1) Improvised story line and situations.
2) Use of the Commedia character types and costumes
3) Slapstick humor and Lazzi bits.
4) Travelling family troupes.
5) Women playing female roles.
6) No permanent stage.

Basket lazzi in a modern musical with a Commedia dell'arte format: **Sganarelle's Secret**, book and lyrics by T. Torp, music by J. Spinetti and based on a play by Moliere. Note that none of these modern performers wear masks but the travelability of their costumes, props and set are evident. Sganarelle's (Arlecchino) slapstick is also worth note.

Chapter Eight
The Renaissance

Rebirth and New Discoveries

Renaissance means "re-birth", but in the history of theatre it was more of a rediscovery. When Constantinople fell to the Turks in 1453, Rome regained importance as the center of the Western civilization. Artifacts and manuscripts of Greek and Roman antiquity were rescued from the Eastern invasion and came under a new scrutiny. No longer were they regarded as relics of a pagan and therefore inferior culture. In 1465 the printing press was introduced in Italy and by 1470 the plays of Terence had been translated and published. Staging these classic dramas soon followed.

Italian nobility was responsible for this new outlook and the resultant surge of artistic production was under their new patronage. It was a reflection on the high status of a prince to sponsor and collect great art. Artists of all types were jealously sponsored and the magnificance of their output became an advertisement for the city, region, or prinicpality. And of course its ruler. What resulted was a series of new innovations in production, writing, performing, and just plain looking at the world which in their day seemed to be a rebirth, but were independently inventive and influential to a degree that is still with us. The proscenium theatre building, the theoretical dramatic rules of neo-classicism, the gentrification of acting and inclusion of women, the invention of opera and its wide dissemination are products in the world of theatre of this pride of patronage.

Let's begin with the theatre building itself. Most modern theatre structures are architecturally inventions of the Renaissance proscenium stage. And the proscenium stage itself was the result of two innovations of the Renaissance nobility staging. Rather than reconstruct the Greco-Roman buildings around them the theatrical entrepreneurs who were setting out to stage classic drama for the wealthy looked for space in the Noble prince's sumptuous palaces. A ballroom, banquet hall, or, since the indoor sport of tennis had began to wane in popularity, a tennis court was converted for the event. These supplied an enclosed rectangular level space with a good floor and some upper galleries for additional viewing. The Prince and his party could be comfortably enthroned at one end with a good view of the stage platform set across the dance floor. The form of our present theatres was thus arrived at not through Greek models, though some of that terminology was retained.

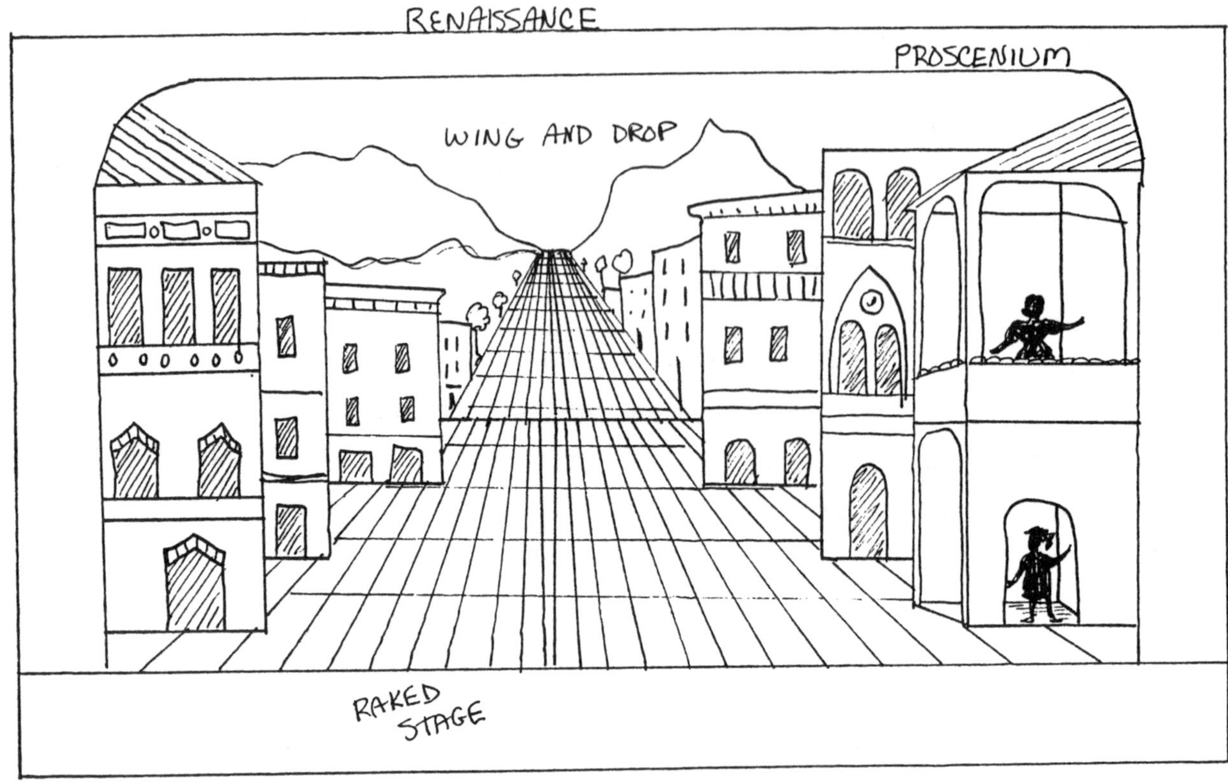

The **proscenium arch** (remember the classic pro-scena?) which came to be a standard and dominant feature of these theatres and thus our own, came about from necessity of an aesthetic nature. It was a result of the invention of that clever artistic illusion which we call **perspective drawing**. We take it so for granted that it is not possible for us to imagine the almost magical effect its principles and application had on the artistic world of the Renaissance. In simple flat two-dimensional lines retreating to a vanishing point established by the artist, a whole world of illusionary distance and three dimensional forms took shape. When applied to staging with forced reduction in buildings retreating from the audience, with a raked stage floor to add to the mirage, and of course careful grouping of actors down front away from the phoniness of the reduced distance (although some wealthy patrons hired midgets to stand in the background to give the illusion of normal people in the distance!) the effect to an audience must have been awesome. One thing was needed, however, to complete the illusion: a frame for the picture. Named the proscenium, this frame concealed the rough edges and off stage support system. The proscenium arches also took on an elaborate decorative function which they still maintain.

To reproduce this three dimensional illusion on a flat surface the scene designer of the Renaissance developed three devices: side wings, back drops, and overhead borders. The wings consisted of flat shutters or painted panels mounted from front to back of the stage at the sides of the acting area. They were grouped in series and could be slid along slots in the stage floor or suspended overhead racks. By simply pulling aside one set the painted surfaces behind could be revealed, causing an exciting and almost instantaneous change of locale. We still use the label "wings" to denote the side areas of the stage which these flats concealed, and an actor who goes on stage unprepared and has to refer to his lines and cues from offstage left or right is still said to be "winging it."

The **drop** was a flat painted curtain stretched smooth or framed tight. These were also in series so they could be raised or "flown" into the overhead space which was labelled **the flies**. Carefully painted in conjunction with the wing pieces, this back drop concealed the back wall of the stage and still presented a limitless vista to the audience. Still used extensively for outdoor scenes in modern theatres this type of setting is called "wing and drop" scenery.

The third element necessary were overhead strips associated with each group of wing flats to conceal the fly space from audience scrutiny. These were called **borders**.

Actors could enter or exit from between the groups of wing pieces at the sides of the stage. They also could be flown in by use of elaborate flying tackle suspended in the flies and concealed by the borders. Because of the speed of shutter action miraculous discovery scenes were also possible. And the proscenium arch afforded a wonderful opportunity to suspend a front curtain.

Because the stage floor was raked or slanted up away from the audience to assist in the perspective illusion and because it often contained slots to slide the wing pieces along, the actors seldom performed up among this scenery but in front of it on a flat **forestage** or **apron**. The rake did give us more acting terminology, however. To walk away from the audience meant literally to go up hill on this stage. Thus: **upstage**. To come toward the audience was to come **downstage**. Because getting higher up and behind your fellow actors was a device used to "steal" a scene it became known as **upstaging**.

The Academies

Revivals of the classic comedies of Terence and Plautus were given elaborate staging at Noble weddings, royal visitations and events of civic pride. Another series of performances developed under the auspices of the Italian **Academies** formed at this time. Scholastic in purpose, these fraternal groups took areas of classical study as their responsibility and exerted their group efforts to investigation and reconstruction of what could be gathered together about this area from the past. One of the first subjects to find influential discourse was an interest in literary theory. Almost from the time of its publication in Latin translation in 1498, Aristotle's treatises particularly **the Poetics**, became the dominant voice in this study. As we already know Aristotle's writings are open to many interpretations. The Academicians, however, tended to see them as hard and fast rules which knowing individuals seeking perfection in their art could not break. These so called rules were to have an effect on playwriting well into the eighteenth century. They formed the core for what became known as **Neo-classicism**.

The Rules

These so-called "rules" produced no great dramatic works during the Renaissance. Their effects will be discussed in later chapters as they began to influence playwrights. It is worthy of our study, however, to list them now as they were first set forth at this time. The basic principles of this neo-classicism can be listed as: verisimilitude; purity of form; five act format; decorum; functions of drama; the three unities.

1) The principle of **verisimilitude** imposed what critics felt was the "appearance of truth" in all aspects of the drama. This ruled out anything that

could not happen in real life. The supernatural, the fantastic were to be shunned.

2) Only **two legitimate forms** of drama were acceptable: comedy and tragedy. Anything else was mixed form or impure. Comedy was to concern itself with middle or low class people. Tragedy, taking its cue from Aristotle's use of the word "noble" must feature characters who were rulers or nobility.

3) All regular drama was to be written in five act form.

4) **Decorum** concerned itself with **norms** of human behavior. All characterization was to be concerned not with abberations of behavior but with stock patterns set by age, sex, profession and rank.

5) The function of drama was "to teach and to please." Drama could only be legitimized as a literary form if it taught a moral lesson. This led eventually to the need in later centuries for "poetic justice" as a proper end to a play.

6) The three unities were extreme interpretations of Aristotle. **Unity of time** restricted the action to a brief span of events. **Unity of place** presupposed that an audience would not accept wide jumps in locale during the course of a play. **Unity of Action** demanded only one course of action, no subplots. These critical restrictions grew out of the academics and their research-proud need to arbitrate standards in all the arts. It took the Romantic revolution and the advent of Realism in the Nineteenth century to break them down, as we shall see.

Actors and Actresses

The nature of these productions sponsored by the academics and the structure associated with the noble festival performances allowed their performers to gradually make inroads in the age old stigma attached to their trade. Actors too could be acknowledged artisans. With royal patronage they could become respected and respectable citizens. The Nobility themselves loved to indulge in these theatrics, which also helped gain respectability. One did not criticize the Queen and her ladies when they costumed themselves as goddesses and rode an elaborate pageant wagon, or recited dramatic verses and danced on the ballroom floor at the climax of the play. These splendid events, called **Intermezzi**, or **Masques** in England, lent all the respectability of tremendous wealth, professional staging and the royal seal of approval upon what the Medieval church had tried so long to brand sinful.

It also saw the acceptance of women completely as performers. Intermezzi required female dancers, soprano singers, and the wearing of physically revealing attractive costumes. Women filled the bill. Of course they were already accepted in the public performance of Commedia. But now they had found royal patronage. First on the Continent and then after the Restoration in England, the ladies gained their accepted foothold on the stages of the Western World.

It was the invention of an entirely new dramatic form that was to be the Renaissance academies' longest lasting influence. And this very same "invention" became responsible for the widespread popularization of all these other innovations already discussed in this chapter. We call this new form **Opera**.

Invention of Opera

The invention came about as an accident, but it was the result of a scholarly attempt at reconstruction. In 1595 the scholars and musicians of the Camerata, an Academic society in Florence, Italy, set about to reconstruct and stage a classic Greek drama. The rules for this original attempt were obvious from research: 1) a mythological story told 2) in poetic dialogue with 3) a musical accompaniment. Of course 4) a chorus was required and 5) long dramatic solo arias and 6) danced interludes. Though all of these are recognizable from our study of the Greek theatre, their combination and manipulation by the Renaissance musicians and their followers resulted not in a museum reproduction, but the vibrant new art form we call opera. And this art form was immensely popular. Every court in Italy had to stage them to prove it was abreast of the new wave in art. Soon this spread throughout Europe. In 1637, a public opera house opened in Venice and the common people took up the craze.

More than the Opera as a form was being popularized. Of course each courtly manor, each public opera house had to have "Italian" staging, "Italian" music, "Italian" performers. Proscenium houses, complete with wing and drop staging machinery, were constructed all over the Continent; many are still standing and in some, such as that in the Queen's summer palace in Drottningholm, Sweden, the machinery still functions! Italian poets writing **liberetti** or books written according to the rules of neo-classicism were in demand. Composers were expected to visit Italy to absorb the Italian methods of opera writing. Italian singers and performers, especially the exotic castrati, who specialized in the leading roles in these operas, demanded huge salaries and developed huge fanatic followings. Their influence spread the public's growing respect for the actor's trade.

Like the Commedia dell'Arte, the Renaissance did not leave a dramaturgy that is still staged. Its importance is in the discoveries and then influence on later ages. Such as:

1) Translating and printing classical sources: Aristotle, Plautus, Terence, Seneca, Vitruvius.
2) The proscenium theatre and wing and drop staging.
3) Rules of neo-classicism.
4) Spread of respect for actors and actresses.
5) Opera.

Like its Renaissance predecessor the Opera, Musical Comedy has become overwhelmingly the most popular form of theatre in this century. And at the same time the most expensive to produce. This scene from **Kismet** by Wright and Forest illustrates the spectacles and fantasy at the root of both forms. The singers are grouped in openly presentational manner. The raised arms are a traditional convention of the musical stage, signalling the end of a musical number and requesting applause from the audience.

Chapter Nine
Two Titans of the Theatre

The Sixteenth and Seventeenth Centuries

In the two centuries that followed this re-awakening in Italy, two European playwrights emerged of such titanic genius and continuing popularity that their influence has come to dominate the span of this chapter of theatrical history. Their schooling in theatre practice and its results in their dramatic writings make a unique comparison and contrast that encapsulated what followed upon those scholarly discoveries that set the Renaissance in motion. At the same time both reflect in their art Medieval practice and Commedia dell'Arte influences. Each is very much a product of his homeland and the dynamic it played in that age of discovery, invention, and world wide exploration. Most critics acknowledged that Shakespeare is England's greatest playwright and that Moliere is France's.

William Shakespeare was born in 1564 in the small English town of Stratford. There he spent the first twenty years of his life as the son of a successful glove maker who was prominent in town political and social life holding the offices of Baliff and then Alderman. Young William was schooled in the traditional Latin literature (Plautus was the school model for comedy; Seneca, for tragedy) and Anglican church-approved Biblical studies, which in the traditional schooling methods of those days would have been set to rote memorization. As he matured, married, and established a family in the small town atmosphere, he must have also experienced local fairs, royal celebrations for the Queen on her progression through the territory and of course performances by the many travelling acting companied who passed through the town when summer and plague months forced them out of London and the larger English cities.

Shakespeare in London

Sometime in his middle twenties, William left his wife and family in Stratford and journeyed to London to become an actor in one of these companies that had played in his town. The most probable time for this would seem to be 1587, when he was 23, because in that year five different companies of actors performed in Stratford. At any rate he soon made a name for himself in London.

First he gained note in the the difficult trade of acting. In Elizabethan theatre practice this was no easily acquired skill. To gain membership in an acting company or troupe usually required a period of apprenticeship to learn all the necessary skills. Actors had to deliver long and eloquent monologues or soliloquys. Their parts required them to duel, fence, wrestle, and fight vigorously and realistically at very close quarters with their audiences so no fakery was possible. Because members of the company were few, and plays sometimes had large cast numbers, every actor had to double in a number of roles within a play. Since masks were no longer used this required rapid and convincing costume and character metamorphosis. Each company performed plays in repretory set up. This requires an actor to hold in store many major and minor characterizations: lines as well as actors. New plays were continuously being written or old favorites being revised and so a quick wit and ability to memorize were needed.

Popularity of the acting companies in London developed a ready market for play scripts. There Shakespeare soon became even more adept. By the time he retired from the theatre and returned to Stratford in 1612, he had written thirty-six plays and parts of others. His writings also included several long story poems and a privately circulated poetry collection.

To assure himself a share of the company profits he had become a fellow or partner in a company of actors formed around the popular actor Richard Burbage. Under the patronage of the Lord Chamberlain this company not only became the most popular and therefore profitable company in London, but also entered into an equally successful ownership of its own theatre, the Globe. Later still they opened a unique indoor performance space: The Blackfriars.

Prestige and profits from these theatrical and literary endeavors allowed Shakespeare to be granted a noble coat of arms and to purchase land and real estate in and around Stratford as well as in London, and he died a comfortably well-off and widely respected Englishman.

English Production before 1640

Aside from the undeniable and unfathomable fact of the man's genius the events of his life can present us with most of the data necessary to understand theatrical practice in England immediately after the Renaissance was felt there. First of all we see that performance had passed beyond the need for an occasion (religious festival in Greek; holiday event in Rome; church pagaent in the Middle Ages; Royal wedding on the Continent) and had became a frequent and continuing source of public entertainment. We see that performances were in the hand of companies of professional actors who sometimes located in major cities but were always ready and expected to tour and perform in a variety of locations. One hold-over from Medieval practice was the still enforced stigma against women on the stage. Young boys, usually apprenticed to older actors, performed all female roles in the play. Unlike the Greek practice however, and in keeping with Medieval sensibility which made believability a necessity, the boys were skilled in the art of female impersonation.

Scripts did not belong to their authors but to the company which purchased them on an outright payment basis. They could be rewritten and revised without recourse to the original writer and black market printed copies were a fact of everyday practice and a source of concern since they allowed a rival company to present its own version of a profitable play. Thus original scripts were jealously guarded by the owning company and printing the text was understandably delayed until a play had worn out its performance span.

The influence of the Renaissance on these play scripts was more in the Latin models chosen than in any theoretic approach to playmaking. The Neo-classic rules were not a force in Shakespeare's England as they came to be on the Continent. Therefore tragic and comic elements blend together in the plays although the tragic elements are usually restricted to a character who represents nobility and the comic element in the tragedies are supplied by lower class characters. The plays were printed in five act form but no act divisions were necessary in performances which proceeded nonstop because there was no curtain or lighting devices. The plays often featured a prologue character, however; and they concluded by the actors dancing a lively jig.

According to Renaissance standard the plays were also written in verse. In England this soon developed into **Blank Verse**, an unrhymed verse form of even lines of Iambic Pentameter, a rhythmic speech form with five stressed syllables to a line. Often the final two lines of a scene would be rhymed. The plays, both tragic and comic also featured interspersed songs, and allegorical characters. Some of these seem to owe their origin to Medieval morality plays or to the Intermezzi of the Italian academies.

The Senecan model set the standard in tragedy. Single minded villainy and the revenge play held center stage. Gruesome and horrific events were staged as realistically as possible. An actor spat out a piece of raw liver to effect the gory event of a character biting out his own tongue in a popular play by Shakespeare's contemporary Thomas Kyd. But no trace of the three unities is evident. Plays range over a long time span, a world wide locale from scene to scene, and subplots abound.

Comedies follow the Plautine pattern. Domestic tangles, parent-child disputes, lost and found children and in some cases even to direct story line from one of the model comedies will be used by an Elizabethan playwright, but with much embellishment. Shakespeare, for example, adds a second set of twins to Plautus' **Menaechmi** when he adapts it into **The Comedy of Errors**. Another strong influence on Shakespeare and his countrymen were the improvisation and character types of the Commedia. Who else is Falstaff if not that braggart Capitano?

There also appeared a third form of play called the Romance. These were neither tragedies nor comedies but long melodramatic tales of separated lovers' trials and tribulations before being reunited. Most of Shakespeare's last plays fit into this mixed category which the Neo-classic rules could not recognize.

Of course Latin plays abounded in elaborate word play, long rhetorical set speeches, and pithy sententia. Elizabethan playwrights delighted in these same literary extravagances. They also seem to have delighted in the ability to use as wide a vocabulary as possible, often inventing new terms of expression as well as using a variety of foreign quotations.

The theatre buildings in England at this time were also a wide departure from the stages designed for use on the Continent. Taking as their model the open courtyards of inns where they performed in London and on tour, or the example of the round bull and bear bating arenas, the Globe and its rivals the Rose, the Curtain, the Swan, the Fortune and even the first of them all called simply the Theatre, were simple wooden structures built around an open courtyard called "the pit." The audience stood in this area to view the play or paid extra pennies to go up into the rings of galleries that overlooked this space and allowed an overhead covering from the thatched roof as well as benches to sit on. The stage was a platform thrusting into the pit from one side. It also was roofed over by "the heavens" which allowed machinery for flying to be concealed above the acting area. The platform itself had trap doors for the devil and ghosts to appear and disappear. Behind the stage were curtained areas and of course the galleries above it could be used for balcony scenes or musicians. Despite the wide ranging nature of the play scripts very little scenery seems to have been used. Surviving inventories of the company managers seems to indicate only bare necessities of furniture, thrones, wall hangings, banners, etc. And the plays themselves are rich in descriptive language which serves to paint the background for an imaginative audience.

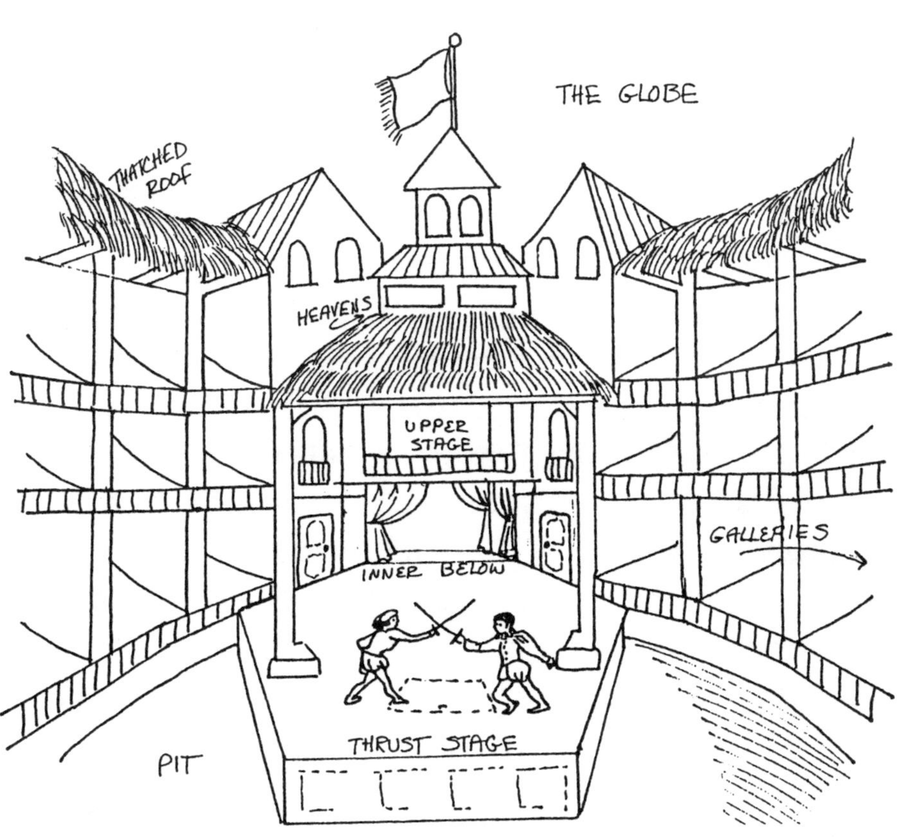

The puritanical control of London's city government prevented any of these theatres from being built within the city walls, so all of them were in outlying districts. Most were across the Thames and required a boat trip. To signal performances the theatres flew a flag from its topmost roof peak. Royal patronage and popular support kept these theatres busy despite the religious backlash, and a wealth of great writers in addition to Shakespeare, Kyd, Dekker, Webster, Marlowe, and Ben Jonson produced an unequaled number of still produced plays. Unfortunately the great flowering of the theatre came to an abrupt standstill when Cromwell and his Roundheads overcame the Royalist troops in the Civil War and in 1642 the theatres were closed and torn down. When performances resumed in 1660 with the Restoration a whole new set of practices and playscripting was brought over from the Continent where Charles II's court had been in refuge. So the theatre of Shakespeare and his cohorts was superseded by the French model.

Moliere in Paris

Jean-Baptiste Poquelin, known to history as Moliere, was born in 1622 in the burgeoning French city of Paris. There he spent the first twenty years of his life as the son of a successful upholsterer and furniture maker who was prominent enough to be appointed Valet to the King, Louis XIII. Young Jean-Baptiste was schooled in a traditional parish school and then sent to the College of Clermont where under the tutelage of the Jesuits he read widely in philosophy as well as the Latin writings of Plautus and Terence, and the lives of the saints. He received a degree in law and jurisprudence but seems never to have put it into practice. Living in Paris, however, he would have been open to a wealth of theatrical experiences. Cardinal Richelieu, the power behind Louis XIII's throne, had set out to make France the cultural center of Europe and of course Paris was its crown jewel. In his private palace the Cardinal built the first proscenium theatre in France in 1641 and imported a company of Italian comedians to perform there. But there were several companies already functioning in theatres about town. Then, too, there were fairs and booth theatre, travelling mountebank showmen, and of course royal spectacles sometimes open to the public. In 1636 occurred an event which would have influenced much discussion and notoriety among scholarly and philosophical circles. Pierre Corneille, a popular playwright, achieved his great success with a historical tragedy called **The Cid**. Though it was written in five act verse form, it violated some of the rules of Neo-classicism according to the French Academy, a group supposed to contain the forty most eminent literary minds of the day. The debate which resulted eventually served to make the "rules" the legitimate standard for dramaturgy from then on.

In his early twenties Jean-Baptiste assumed the name of Moliere and formed a company of shareholding performers (they referred to themselves as "Children of the Family.") with the popular comic actress Madeleine Bejart as star attraction. Failing to find a Parisian audience they set out on the road, touring the French province for fifteen years before they returned. During this extended tour the young man developed his craft the way his English counterpart had.

First he gained note as an actor. French theatre practice, like the English, was a demanding trade. Vocal and physical skills were required as well as memorization and retention of many roles played in repertory. Since companies tended to specialize in tragedy or comedy, however, this somewhat lightened the chore. Also Moliere usually played the lead part and therefore was not required to double in other parts. Fights and battle scenes were usually offstage events as well, but comic lazzi as practiced by the Commedia dell'Arte companies was a skill to be mastered by any actor or actress.

While in the country Moliere also began to write plays to bolster the meager repertoire of his little company. Using Plautine patterns and scripted Commedia-like comic scenes he developed a number of popular comedies that he later revived and revised on his successful return to Paris in 1658.

In Paris his company was assigned by the new king Louis XIV to share the stage, alternating evenings, of the Petit Bourbon with the Italian actors. They acted under the patronage of the King's brother, the Duc d'Orleans. Before his death in 1673 he can be credited with more than thirty plays. Comic masterpieces, some Plautine and farce driven, others lofty social satire written in delicate verse couplets. His attempts at serious drama all failed and he produced no other literary forms with the exception of a few prose "after pieces" or staged satirical debates on theatrical matters. He also embellished the scenarios of elaborately staged ballets or intermezzi in which the sun king particularly delighted. Despite the popularity of his plays and the universal acknowledgement of his acting superiority all of his work was subject to extreme censorship by the Royal family as well as the Academy experts. One play, **Tartuffe**, was withheld from production for years because its theme of religious hypocrisy offended the King's mistress. Even though he was in the patronage of the Royal family, the anathema of the Catholic church held force and on his death he could not be granted religious rites nor buried in consecrated ground.

Production in France during the Seventeenth Century

As in the case of his English counterpart, the facts of the life of this French master playwright give us insight into the theatrical practices of his own milieu and era. Though popular theatre was to be found everywhere and needed no special occasion, the Royal family demand's and noble events continued to commission new productions. In contrast, in England Queen Elizabeth merely requested that Shakespeare's players put on for her an already established production from the Globe. Although her successor King James did commission Ben Jonson to write original amateur ballet-like spectacles or Masques.

No Medieval stigma against female actors here in France, either. Women, as we see from the example of Madeleine Bejart, were often the proud center of an acting company as they always were in the Commedia dell'Arte troupes.

Scripts were here the property of the company as well, but unlike England there seems not to have been such concern over nor much of a market in bootleg printed scripts. Perhaps the strict control on production handed down by the Academy and Royal authority now in the hands of Cardinal Mazarin were responsible for this.

As we know strict enforcement also had its effect on playwriting. Comedy and tragedy could not be mixed as Shakespeare and his English counterparts so readily delighted in doing. The models were still Plautus and Terence, with the latter influencing refined language and a more delicate sense of human foibles taking precedance over rough and tumble Plautine farce which was considered crude and unrefined. Senecan tragedy was copied for its rhetorical analysis of human sins, but the more flagrant bloody scenes were not duplicated, although the French wrote glorious death scenes for their tragic actors and actresses. The plays were printed in five act form with some French scene divisions but of course were performed nonstop. Since they were performed indoors, elaborate candle light effects could be utilized and a curtain was possible.

Though some of Moliere's farces were in prose, most plays of the period were written in verse couplets making them extremely difficult to translate into English without sounding either sing-song or just plain precious. The plays also attempted to adhere to the three unities. Setting is usually not mentioned at all, but left to a vague "somewhere in the house or castle" sort of approach. And time is sometimes sandwiched into the span of one day without any recourse to realistic explanation. To reinforce the verisimilitude of action and character the confidante is supplied so that characters in the play can speak their minds without the artificiality of a soliloquy.

Like Shakespeare, Moliere adapted Plautus to his needs reworking **The Pot of Gold** into **The Miser**. And he readily borrowed Commedia dell'Arte characters and situations for many of his plays although he changed names, remaking Harlequin as Sganarelle or Scapin. His compatriots, the great writers of tragedy Racine and Corneille, took their plots directly from the classic myths or historical or Biblical writings which they used not to illustrate swashbuckling action as the English did, but to present characters in refined rhetorical self analysis of the finer points of the emotional conflict.

The theatres used by the middle of the seventeenth century in France were all proscenium houses equipped in the Italian manner. Once Moliere stopped touring the only exception to this would have been to the large outdoor spaces where some of the ballet-musical productions were performed. But this also included wing and drop arrangements, candelabra stage lights and a raised stage at one end of a long rectangular space. Scenery for these opera-like productions could be elaborate and spectacular and was expected to be changed in full view of the audience. Costumes worn by the actors and actresses were always in the style of the day, not historically accurate. And as in England an occasional touch might indicate an exotic time period: plumes in a headdress, or a sash to suggest a Roman toga.

It was this form of playwriting and production, along with a strict overseeing of the theatre though the issuance of "patents" that Charles II brought back from France when he was restored to the monarchy in England. From that time, strict division of comedy and tragedy, indoor proscenium stage, and women on those stages became standard expectancy. Unlike Shakespeare's broad all-inclusive comedy the Restoration wits specialized in a refined, Continental comedy of social manners. Their plays were written for the socially elite and held up to scorn the lower classes and the religiously zealous. They illustrated a world like that of Plautus with little concern for morality but with a sharp sense of satirical wit and an eye for the ridiculous in human behavior. Restoration tragedy writers abandoned the free flowing blank verse of the Elizabethans and wrote in a a rhymed couplet form like the French.

Reading a Shakespearean Play

1. Remember that act and scene divisions are a printer's convention, the play is one continuous action.
2. Sub plots are almost always a mirror of the main plot ,used to give added insight into what the play is about.
3. Soliloquies were intended to tell what the character really thinks. No Freudian subtext was intended.
4. The playwright, his actors and his audience loved words, all kinds of words, so enjoy them. Read out loud if you can.
5. In most cases stage directions have been added by later editors.
6. Much of Shakespeare's genius is due to his warm observation of the humanity in all his characters. No villain is totally evil; no comic character is completely ridiculous.

Reading a Moliere Play

1. As in Shakespeare the play is one continuous action.
2. Since the plays were written for specific actors the characters tend to have physical quirks associated with the original performer. Moliere uses his own throat-clearing habit, another's stammer, etc.

3. Presentational devices are often used, such as a character directly addressing the audience.
4. Commedia-like physical action must be imagined at times to spark the humor present in the words of the script.
5. Don't expect subplots, all characters relate to the main action. But the comedies often feature a "Deus ex Machina" ending.

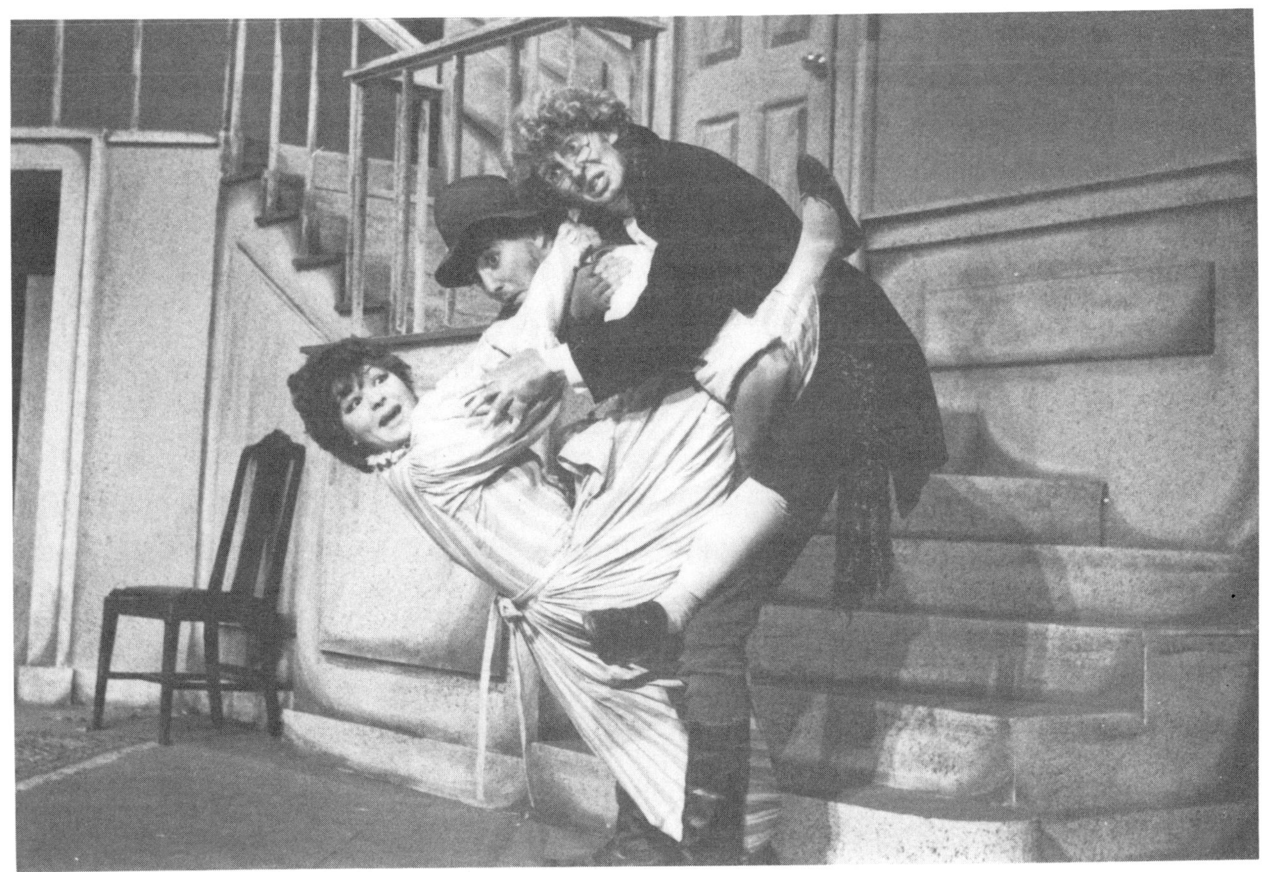

A modern production of Moliere's great comedy **The Miser** here catches the central character Harpagon in an openly Commedia dell'arte-esque bit of physical humor with two of his zany servants. Note that like most contemporary stagings of Moliere and Shakespeare, the director and designers have moved the time of the play to one more understandable to a modern audience. In this case the high wigs and petticoat britches of the French 17th century are foregone for the Victorian era to make use of the audience's familiarity with the times of that other famous miser: Ebenezer Scrooge.

Chapter Ten
Theatre in Transition

The first half of the eighteenth century in Europe was an age of Reason, or as the German labelled it: The Enlightenment. It was a time perfectly suited to the rules of Neo-classicism and their insistence on adherence to logic, decorum, and verisimilitude. But within this search for truth lay the beginnings of a revolt that forced this very order to give way to the onslaught of Romanticism. While theatres on the Continent continued to follow the French models of Racine in tragedy and Moliere in comedy, the English spread out in new directions.

Production methods were standardized in the Italian mode, but the playwright increasingly came under pressure from the Church of England to justify the more salacious comedy and openly cruel satire of conventional morality that was a standard feature of the sophisticated Restoration plays. What developed came to be known as **Sentimental Comedy**: plays with a happy ending that featured long, tearful trials borne bravely by their protagonists. Rooted as they were in Shakespearean romances, they also became precursors for the popular Melodramas of the following century. Some playwrights held out to write what they called "laughing comedy." Sheridan and Goldsmith's plays in this style are still performed, but the tearful comedies of their contemporaries are forgotten. So began the breakdown of logic and the doctrine of "to teach and to please" as a standard for playwrights.

B.O. = Beggars' Opera and Box Office

In 1728 a so-called "ballad opera" called the Beggars Opera, written by John Gay, opened at the little Theatre Royal in Lincoln's Inn Fields outside of London and became an overnight success. It went on to become the most popular show of the century, being revived every year from then on. Companies performed it all over England, in Ireland, on the Continent, and even in America. Its influence, in addition to its popularity, was far reaching as well. Gay had conceived it as a take-off on Italian opera, which was at that time the most popular entertainment form in England under the aegis of the King's favorite composer,. Handel. With a company of singers imported from Italy, including several world reknowned castrati for masculine lead roles, Handel was firmly established at the Royal Academy of Music to which the public flocked for each new opera he wrote.

The Beggar's Opera purported to be a similar work by and featuring performers from London's street rabble, thieves and whores. It featured all the traditional popular situations of the high toned opera: jealous women, valiant men, a prison scene, a wedding ceremony, a thwarted execution, a tearful begging daughter, and of course a "deus ex machina" miraculous happy rescue at the end. But all of this was set not in a fantasy Greek or Roman past, but in the slums of London.

The musical score also satirized operatic conventions. Two divas battled both vocally and physically for the audience and the hero at the same time. A chorus of men and another of women had musical scenes, but the men were a band of highwaymen dividing their loot, and the women's scene was in a whorehouse! Instead of lofty original music the playwright chose street ballads and popular songs and ditties of the day and set original words to them that were often the opposite of what the original expressed. Add to all of this novelty a layer of political satire (the hero, a highwayman in a thinly disguised double for the King's Prime Minister) and Gay had a controversial but resounding success.

Almost at once it had an effect on performance practice. Its great popularity allowed it to be performed over and over night after night (an unheard of 62-night run that first year alone!), a phenomenon that was to replace the repertory system eventually with our present long run policy. It developed such a number of other "ballad operas" that the Italian opera lost audiences, forcing Handel to turn to writing non-theatrical works such as **Messiah**, his great oratorio. Though none of these imitators have achieved any lasting popularity, it was the original's use of musical satire and popular tunes that led to the nineteenth century successes of Gilbert and Sullivan in operetta form and even serve as a model for many American musicals of the present century. Sentimental comedy, which had also been a target of the satire began to decline in popularity along with the Opera.

The Romantic Revolution

The second half of the eighteenth century and the first half of the nineteenth century were marked by revolutions. The American fight to liberate itself from English rule set off a series of wars of political liberation in the Old World as well as the New. James Watt's energy dynamo the steam engine sparked what was to become the Industrial Revolution. And in the arts came the liberating battles of the Revolt of Romanticism which would defeat the Neo-classic ideals.

Begin with a philosophical and religious movement called **Transcendentalism**. Founded on the belief that God had created the universe out of himself in order to contemplate himself, this posed the view that all natural things were related, and man as a part of nature was related to all being. To learn about God one need only study all natural things or for that matter to learn of one's self one could contemplate nature. But, only if nature was unaltered or unshaped by the forces of "civilization." Neo-classicists of the eighteenth century had sought to train and restrict nature to their standard of beauty: geometric flower beds, carefully cropped lawns, topiary trimmed trees and bushes. They pulled up the carriage blinds when crossing the Alps so as not to see the "ugly" mountains. Romanticists on the other hand saw beauty in wild and desolate moors and stormy oceans, craggy rock outcroppings and gnarled old trees.

These notions of what was natural and therefore beautiful altered the Romantic artists' view of the world around them and this had a lasting effect on their art. Rules were now restrictions that had to be broken in order to achieve the true essence or natural beauty. And that unique individual who could not be restrained was labelled the **Genius**. He was ahead of his time, unappreciated until after his death, and of course an eccentric in behavior and dress, since no rules applied to him. The art he produced had a rough unfinished quality but its genius put it above criticism. In theatre Shakespeare again became the great standard because Romantic artists saw his plays as great unshaped works of art. The very lack of obedience to the rules which Neo-classicists decried in his work now became virtues. Hamlet was not just a troubled young prince but a misunderstood genius.

Another character created by the Romantic mind was the **Noble Savage**. Man in his wild, uncivilized state was by nature good and perfect. Missionaries and colonizers, even the best intentioned ones, brought only crime and corrupting influences of commercial life, to say nothing of their diseases into these Eden-like natural utopias. The country bumpkin, who had been the target of eighteenth century scorn, now became a natural, uncomplicated hero. Sir Walter Scott's valiant Highlanders and James Fenimore Cooper's new world frontiersmen were protagonist models in the new drama of Romanticism.

With this admiration for the wild and untamed came also a fascination with the exotic and particularly the Oriental. A strong influence in Romantic art came from Chinese, Japanese, Indian, and Moorish sources. Tales of the Arabian Nights, fantastic folk tales, all of which of course were mirrored in Shakespeare's later plays, became dramatic fodder.

Two other trends fed this love of exoticism. The nationalistic movement in politics and art spread to each corner of Europe with the breakup of Napolean's dream of a united European kingdom. Scandinavians, Russians, and Germans mined their own folk tales and folk arts and crafts for heroic and dramatic ore. The past, particularly the Medieval ages, caught the imagination of Romantic artists; castles and cathedrals became the setting of many nineteenth century dramas. And then to free the mind of eighteenth century nationalism the Romantics embraced the irrational. Ghosts, spirit presences, witches and fairies, trolls and monsters, all forms of folk and legend induced fantasy from the unreal world returned to the art of the new rebels. Of course here too Shakespeare supplied abundant models.

Underneath and permeating it all was a strong strain of deep religious sentiment. If man was basically good one needed only to remove the civilizing forces of society and its demands to reveal God's creature. Romantic drama saw no irony in the miraculous conversion of the villanous antagonist at the final curtain.

Playwriting

Plays now could flood the stage with crowd scenes, battle fields, wide time and place shifts and a plethora of subplots. The five act format and use of poetic language particularly for serious drama held out until the realistic outlook limited its use at the end of the century. An interesting development in the playwright's status was the gradual assumption of national copyright protection resulting in the International Copyright Law of 1887. By the turn of the present century playwrights could reasonably expect protection of their work and a reasonable profit from productions, as well as printed texts in their own country and abroad.

The classic Romantic drama reached its peak of popularity in the form of the America melodrama. The stage adaptation of Harriet Beecher Stowe's anti-slavery novel, **Uncle Tom's Cabin**, was the most widely performed and imitated in this genre.

Production Needs of Romantic Drama

Theatrical performances, which became the major source of entertainment for all classes during the Romantic era, naturally began to demand ever larger performance spaces. As national companies were formed throughout the Continent, new venues were constructed in the proscenium arch equipped opera house design, suitable of spectacular stage effects and large audiences. More and more realistic natural scenic background came into demand and the new technology strove to keep up. Gas lights and then electric lighting allowed the many outdoor scenes in the new plays to glow like nature's own. Lime light and then the carbon arc allowed beams of light to be cast from a distance. Cut-out drops from forests eventually included three dimensional rocks and trees. Smoke machines, overhead rocking troughs for snowfall, transparent scrim curtains added to the duplication of natural effects. Cannonballs rolling down wooden racks rumbled like real thunder. Treadmills for real horses to race on, trapdoors and flying harnesses for ghosts, even tanks of water onstage for lakes and rivers were part of the spectacle equipment of these stage houses. The great number of theatre fires caused by all of this resulted in extensive safety technology as well. A fire wall at the proscenium and of course an asbestos curtain raised and lowered before the show became eventually as standard a feature as playing the national anthem for an overture. Since spectacular stage effect was so important, the curtain was now always drawn between acts and to cover staging changes. The **curtain call**, when this curtain was raised again after the conclusion of the play so the audience could admire a tableau, also became a time for actors to come forward and bow to their fans or they might speak a short speech in front of the curtain.

Romantic actors reached a stage of popularity that had not been seen before. A great performer like Sarah Bernhart could go on tour with her own costumes and a few scenic pieces and perform all around the western world using local pick up actors or the local resident company for the other roles. No elaborate rehearsals were needed; the actor merely took center stage and turned on the histrionic fireworks. With popularity also came respect. In 1895 Henry Irving became the first English actor to be knighted.

Melodrama, which was the nineteenth century's most popular theatrical form, was named for the practice of using a musical accompaniment to most scenes. This meant of course that every theatre must have an orchestra pit in front of the stage and hire a group of professional musicians. Music underscored dramatic scenes just as it does in our modern movies or could be used for interspersed songs or folk dances. It also served to fill staging change gaps and played an overture and music for the audience to file out to.

The revival of the popularity of Shakespeare, a phenomenon that is still with us, led to a number of new theatrical ideas. Rather than staging his plays as he had done in contemporary costumes and as the Neo-classicists had insisted in standardized scenery, the Romantic productions began to stress historical research in costuming and background. A sense of historical accuracy that was to become a holy rule for the Realists began to be felt in the theatre as it was in the other arts enamored as they were with the romantic love of the past.

Romanticism has never completely disappeared from the stage nor been banished to the dustbin of old-fashionedness. The concept of Genius, the character of the Nobel Savage, and the distrust of mechanized society are features of plays on Broadway and our college stages now. The great Romantic dramas from **Faust** to **Hernani** live on in opera houses where their musical adaptations are pre-eminent. The melodramatic format dominates most musicals and the popular science fantasy movies.

Reading and Recognizing Romantic Drama

1. Review the characteristics of melodramatic form.
2. There is usually a great star role in the central part, often the play is named for this character.
3. Look for characteristics of the Genius and the Noble Savage.
4. Stage directions are now very important to the playwright. Note particularly long elaborate scenic description particularly of scenes outdoors, on wild mountaintops, or in forests, for example.
5. Folk legends, fairy tales and fantasies usually always fit the mold.
6. A natural cataclysm such as a hurricane or an avalanche serves as a climax.

Poetic language, heroic folk legends, fantasy creatures, magical events, large casts, spectacle and audience grabbing effects. All these features of the Romantic drama are still with us in this age of realism. Here in a scene from Giraudoux's fairy tale play **Ondine** the spirit world of the water sprites looks in on the real domain of the peasant girl and her knight in shining armor. Note the painted texture of the cottage walls in contrast to the real fabrics in the costumes. The costumer also makes use of contemporary hair style and details of clothing as close as possible to current good taste without violating the medieval look. Note also use of modern projected light effect on the cyclorama.

Chapter Eleven
The Modern Theatre

Realism and its Reaction

As we learned in our definition of style and have come to see in our study of historical eras, the validity of art in any age is based on that particular age's view of what is true. Medieval man believing as he did in the timelessness of God's creations failed to recognize anachronisms in his art. Men in the Neo-classic age saw the truth in norms which stripped away excess trivial detail. Modern man, believing as he does in the truth of the scientific method, has come to set "reality" as a standard for his art. What can be experienced by man's five senses (touch, taste, smell, sight and hearing) is what is real. The word "real" has become the key word by which twentieth century man rates his art.

The modern theatre can be dated from the artistic movement called **Realism** originating in Europe in 1860's and 70's. The self-named Realists rejected the fantasy and exoticism of the Romantics and concentrated on the truthful depiction of the common place world they could observe around them. This led to a whole new subject matter in the details of ordinary lives and required a new approach to presentation that allowed an objective view of the everyday world. What it retained from the Romantic view was a continuing study of folk customs and dialect that lent themselves to the realistic love of local color when it went beyond externals and penetrated to character.

Two scientific philosophers were influential in shaping the Realist view: Auguste Comte and Charles Darwin. Comte established Sociology, the study of origins and functions of civilizations and human societies, and believed that knowledge gained through observation must be used to improve society. Darwin's **The Origin of Species**, published in 1859, reduced man to just another natural object, but it presupposed the inevitability of progress and set the "survival of the fittest" doctrine at the heart of all natural observation. Everyone is a product of heredity and environment.

Father of Modern Drama

The Realist movement in theatre owes its continuing impact to the master craftsman of its form, the Norwegian playwright Henrik Ibsen. In his active writing period which spanned the last half of the nineteenth century, Ibsen penned seminal and consummate dramas to which every major theatrical stye of the twentieth century can be traced. Though the first force of his impact was in the Realist vein, the myriad of outgrowths from this, even the many anti-Realist styles which soon sprung up, studied his form, theoretic base and models.

First we can look at him as the master technician among playwrights. The perfection of the **Well-Made Play**, which we have already defined in Chapter 3, is credited to Ibsen, and it is this form which dominates the twentieth century theatre. The well-made play was an invention of the popular French playwright, Eugene Scribe, who along with the equally popular Victorien Sardou wrote more than 400 plays in the format. It was a play of ingenious structure, of clever intrigues, careful presentation, and dramatic climaxes to each act. In order to make the intrigue function, surprising messages delivered in the nick of time, gossiping servants whose only purpose was to set up background facts, and always obvious manipulation of believability became stock in trade to the plays.

Ibsen's genius was to cover the obvious machinery and make it work in purely realistic terms for the audience. The Scribean model almost invariably opened with a butler and dusting maid scene. These two characters served a purely expository function spewing out facts that established place, time, characters, circumstances, even inciting incident. Then they exited never to be seen again and the play went on. Ibsen did not eliminate exposition, he merely disguised it and fragmented it at the same time. Background facts, antecedent action were brought out in a natural manner by having an outsider come in to the scene who could realistically inquire and be answered. Facts were withheld until they would be needed most dramatically. In this way important exposition often occurs in Ibsen's plays in the final act just before the obligatory scene.

Because he usually selects a point of attack very late in the conflict and near the crisis, he can relate each scene to the next in a naturally causal manner and yet maintain a tight suspense of rising action. His plays of the latter period eventually settled into the three act format that has been standard in the twentieth century. Each act was capped with a surprise curtain event and a dramatic curtain line. The final act features an obligatory scene at the crisis which involves the central characters in a discussion which grows realistically out of circumstance and character.

Since every character in the play must be a product of realistic observation, even the maid or handyman is subject in Ibsen to thorough heredity and environment revelation. There are no small parts in his plays, all link into the plot and symbolic fabric. Since the realist was also a dispassionate observer, there are no full-fledged villains or heroes among Ibsen's characters. Dialogue uses folk slang and characterizing idioms but these, like the costume and scenery details described meticulously imprinted copy prepared by the author, have been carefully selected for dramatic reasons.

The well-made play then as Ibsen perfected it came to be: A play of careful preparation where every detail is selected to lead through carefully rising action to a dramatically satisfying climax. Everything that happens is prepared for. We may be surprised by it, but the possibility has been laid out. There are no extraneous facts, events or characters. Asides and soliloquies, all trappings of non-realistic drama are eliminated.

Even without these technical innovations Ibsen's genus shows itself in his ability to understand human beings and present them as living realities on the stage. The wealth of particular detail extended to every character and the keen insight these details reveal make his plays the constant study of twentieth century actors, directors and playwrights. Especially noteworthy is his innovative use of inner dialogue. That is, a second hidden meaning beneath a character's dialogue. Realistic observation was to show, as Ibsen knew even before Freud formulated it, that we often behave and speak in ways we ourselves cannot logically account for. This is now a commonplace in our theatre, but Ibsen first mastered it, and his naturalistic use of this is still unmatched, as is the uncanny depth of human understanding it illustrates.

Serious playwrights as well as writers of comedy were also influenced by Ibsen's insistence on making every play a source of insight to his audience. The thematic structure of his plays leading as it did to a serious discussion was a factor. His depth of character understanding which prevented any one character from being an obvious Raissoneur another. The universality of his concerns and the thoroughness with which he explored them have added to the timelessness of his works. He is also particularly admired among contemporary writers and actors for his deep and compassionate understanding of female characters. He did not like to be classified as either a polemicist or a feminist however. Ibsen merely felt he wrote about human beings and their problems.

Naturalism

One of the first extensions of Realism was a movement in the arts labelled **Naturalism**. Though we see it merely as another more extreme form of realistic theatre, its originator Emile Zola saw in it a distinctly new goal for the arts. Art cannot be shaped into "well-made" packages if it purports to represent real life. Life of common man does not have neatly organized curtain scenes. So if we wish to study man at his most natural we must simply observe a "slice of life." Naturalist plays tried to have no protagonist, instead they are about a group of people and usually a group from the dregs of society,not the top. The closing curtain or point of attack could be arbitrary as was the rambling dialogue and string of sometimes weakly related events. The Naturalists however were pessimistic about man's future. After all, all life ends in death. Therefore Naturalists plays were usually always a tragedy, and they emphasized the sordid aspects of life. The movement in literature was relatively short lived, but its lasting effect has been in production and directing and acting methodology as we will see.

Staging Realist and Naturalist Plays

Since Romanticism and its offspring Melodrama had already developed lighting and staging techniques to a heightened realistic level these inventions were easily applied to the new movement. However, most realistic drama took place indoors, where the environmental influences on relatively fewer characters could be more closely, and therefore scientifically, scrutinized. The result was what came to be standard practice in this century: the three act, one interior set, small cast show. Since scenery was to carefully duplicate real life, wing pieces were now united to the back wall as one continuous surface. Sometimes even a ceiling piece overhead gave the effect of a square room with the wall toward the audience removed. Not a perfect square, however. The side walls had to fan open for purposes of audience sight lines from side seats. But the illusion was one of reality. The result, now standard, was called the **Box Set**.

To add to the illusion realistic light sources were required, so the footlights of the Romantic stage had to go. This also necessitated a change in actor's makeup. The dark eye shadow we now identify with ballet dancers, twenties chorus girls and boys, and movie stars of the silent era, had been a necessity when bright light from below made the eyes appear to bug out of shadowless sockets. It was now replaced with more realistically blended facial cover needed only to retain color and reduce shine under the strong overhead lights.

Where a play did require shifting of scenery from one locale to another mechanical devices were needed because of the extreme weight and accuracy of detail in each set. No longer could moulding, furniture, even landscapes painted on flat surfaces fool the eye of the now realistically attuned audiences.

Mechanical stage elevators capable of lifting whole sets, and turntables adapted from Oriental practice were called to serve. Of course in the realistic theatre all of this shifting was done behind the drawn curtain.

Accuracy in costuming was usually no problem since most realistic plays dealt with the present. Acting, however, had to undergo a complete overhaul from the high flown Romantic style. Natural vocal patterns, eliminating artificial posing, and realistic movement and stage pictures often requiring actors to turn their backs to the audience had to be developed. This led in turn to the necessity of a theatre trained individual who could stand outside the stage picture and control it. The modern director as we know him thus developed.

Naturalism as we have seen pushed realistic playwriting to an extreme. It did the same to staging techniques and it is in this form that its most lasting influence can be felt. Not the illusion of reality, but the actual ultimate reality itself was the Naturalist's goal. In Paris in 1887 Andre Antoine had opened the little Theatre Libre in which he hoped to produce Ibsen and Zola and their followers. Partly from lack of finances with which to build or hire elaborate and expensive stage furniture and props, he borrowed and used his own meager real life possessions. For a scene in a butcher shop he even used real meat. This became a trademark of the Naturalist theatre: use the real thing on stage. Real food, real flowers and plants, real clothes or costumes. David Belasco, the American producer and director went as far as to move three walls of a New York restaurant, plaster, food stains, cockroaches and all, onto a stage for a play that took place in such a restaurant. The stage broke down under the weight of the real thing!

Acting followed suit particularly under the aegis of the Russian actor-director Constantin Stanislavsky. For the actors of the Moscow Art Theatre founded in 1898 he had developed a series of exercises which demanded emotional recall and "living out" of psychological experiences in the life of the actor which would facilitate parallel response in the role on stage. This so-called Stanislavsky Method developed a style of acting that spread throughout the Continent and America. Its extreme exponents sometimes believe they actually live their parts on stage actually becoming that character. They create the illusion of naturalness by stuttering and stammering speeches and a variety of facial and bodily ticks and itches and scratches. Some performers go so far as to actually undress and bathe offstage when a character is supposed to be performing this action, or run around the outside of the theatre when a messenger is required to deliver a message after a long run. The modern movie of course with its ability to film on location, to use real crowd scenes, and to re-shoot action until it gets it right, has made naturalistic effect and acting a standard.

Many critics regard the greatest modern playwright to be Anton Chekhov, the Russian whose plays were first produced by Stanislavsky's company. Written in a deceptively naturalistic style (episodes not clearly related in a plot format, no central character, no clear form since comedy and tragedy are ever present and interactive, vague denouement at fade out), the plays require a carefully rehearsed acting ensemble in which no one actor stands out. This would seem to fulfill the Naturalist manifesto even though the workings of a Ibsenian well-made play can be applied.

The Anti-Realists

As in the other art forms theatre practitioners developed a reaction and backlash to the new realism almost at once. This took many philosophical names and approaches. And the plays of Ibsen were as influential in this anti-realistic movement as they had been in its antithesis. Even in his earliest plays, the large scale dramatic and poetic histories and folk plays in the Romantic mold, Ibsen used symbols to enrich and deepen the plot. Elements of fantasy and the unseen forces at work in everyday lives can be found in the most realistic of his middle period plays and his final works achieve a kind of surreal level of mystery. All these elements became stock in trade to the nonrealistic theatre.

Symbolist Theatre

The first anti-realist movement can best be labelled **Symbolism** although its adherents used many names such as: aestheticism, impressionism, even neo-romanticism. The philosophic basis for these works of art was the belief that one cannot grasp the truth through scientific observation since this only views surface characteristics, not inner spirit. Truth must be conveyed by intuition. Ideas are not conveyed by words but by symbols whose meaning lurks at a greater depth than human linguistics can convey.

Plays of the Symbolist movement revived the use of verse dialogue. Structure broke down into a series of scenes which were often interchangeable. Like the Romantics they tended to return to the past or a fabled landscape apart from the reality of the modern world. Theirs is a world of mysterious and often unexplainable forces. Character's motivation is often left unexplained. Above all the use of all pervading and often repeated symbols gave the genre its name.

Expressionist Theatre

The second major anti-realist movement was called **Expressionism**. It took as its major influence the plays of Ibsen's Swedish contemporary, August Strindberg. Though he started like Ibsen with poetic and romantic drama and then developed into realistic and naturalistic playwriting, it was following a bout with insanity during which he was confined to an asylum, that his writing took a clearly anti-realistic direction. These plays used the viewpoint of a dreamer to allow events to blur together and for time and place to melt. Characters are often nameless and the ever present symbols of the play are often of a highly personal nature to the poet and thus kept secret from the audience.

Expressionist writers who followed on Strindberg's lead as reality as the personal view of the artist. Warped and distorted as this view might be, only the true artist was capable of seeing truth. Thus Expressionist plays feature a central character through whose eyes the audience must view all the action of the play. The world this character sees is a distorted and threatening one. Other characters come and go without names or merely labelled the son, the girl in black, the old man, the gatekeeper, etc. Language is static, sometimes poetic, sometimes bluntly gross, often monosyllabic.

Expressionists especially saw evil in machines, cities, businesses and science. Like their romantic peers they hoped for a return to nature, but they had a strong religious message. Oriental religious ideas and Christ Symbolism are features of both Strindberg and his imitators. The format of Expressionist plays is often a formal series of short scenes progressing, then returning to the starting point in cyclical form. The movement was extremely strong in Germany between the world wars and its effect on staging and the cinema are still felt though the plays of this and the Symbolist movement are not often produced today.

Theatre of the Absurd

A third anti-realist movement, one that still has practitioners, developed in the middle of the twentieth century and came to be known as **Absurdism**. The title comes from the belief that this is essentially an absurd world without logic or meaningful order. Their plays (often labelled anti-plays) are constructed to prove this very sense of chaos and lack of predictability which they see as the reality around them. In so doing, comedy is usually the result and therefore became their strongest mode, but it is a dark and pessimistic comedy at that. It also takes deliberate liberties with the well-made play structure often obviously emphasizing the mechanics of discovery, exposition and crisis.

Each of these movements or "isms" has is equivalent in the other arts. Some of the important twentieth century styles, however, were purely theatrical and remain so today.

Theatricalism might be described as the ultimate realism. It took as its point of departure the belief that in theatre the ultimate reality was the theatre itself. Thus its overriding symbol is the stage and its machinery exposed for the audience to experience. Indeed the audience members themselves become part of the performance and therefore real world of the play. Characters in the plays are more real than the actors who try to portray them. This of course lent itself readily to a dominant staging method much in practice in the last half of this century.

Epic theatre was the invention of one man, the German Bertolt Brecht. It grew out of his conviction that the theatre's main purpose was polemical. He went so far as to insist that plays should not entertain but fire their audiences up with a zeal to go forth and change the world. Primarily a communist manifesto, this urge to preach at one's auditors took the form of many novel and largely presentational devices. Actors stepped out of their roles and harangued the audience. Songs of a chauvinistic nature were inserted without motivation.

Often music presented the opposite mood to the words as when a gentle lullabye is accompanied by strident military march music. The meaning or moral behind each scene is posted on a billboard above the action so the audience can't miss the point being made.

The third form and one that became the dominant force in the twentieth century was the **musical play**. An American invention, the musical owed its roots to the **Beggar's Opera** and its copiers, the comic opera, the operetta and its many forms, and vaudeville performances. It developed along two lines: the dramatic or comic play with musical songs, dances and choruses to forward the plot, and the revue or concept musical which was an interrelated series of skits and songs held together by a theme rather than a plot.

First regarded by many serious critics as a "bastard" and therefore inferior art form, it has by sheer weight of popularity become the dominant form for late twentieth century production and writing. Making use of and helping to extend all of the other styles mentioned above, the musical has at the same time enforces some influence of its own on form. Most musicals are written in a number of scenes but staged with only one intermission. This has further been shortened lately to the one, nonstop performance. Though the naturalists had developed the one-act play form it is only recently and because of musical form that the two act or long one-act play format dominated.

With its emphasis on dance and song as an integral part of plot development the musical strains most noticeably in its attempt to reconcile these presentational devices with the twentieth century's highly representational oriented need for "reality." Subject matter thus stretches to include realistic context by staging scenes in ballrooms or theatres and by choosing plots involving "show biz" events and protagonists who are performers, famous singers or dancers. This also allows the music to act as soliloquy and the dance to express inner thoughts as dream ballet.

Staging the Anti-Realistic Plays

In contrast to their realistic minded colleagues, the anti-realists turned the new mechanics of the theatre to presentational prominence. Exposed light, obtrusive sound, mechanical turntables working in front of the audience have became twentieth century commonplace. And these devices are often openly applied to plays written to be performed in other styles. It has become almost a cliche of the contemporary stage to put Shakespeare's characters in contemporary jumpsuits, exposed flying harnesses, skateboards and of course lit by obvious exposed spot lights.

The Symbolist plays, with their insistence on a mysterious world developed projected scenery and Brecht continued the practice by showing movie backgrounds during scenes in his epic theatre. The scrim, a curtain capable of being lit to appear solid or to melt away revealing a scene behind it, was also a standard of Symbolist and later musical production.

The shifting of scenery in front of the audience without benefit of curtain has also became standard. It added to the fantasy and illusion of Symbolic play, was used for theatrical effect in Theatricalism, and is a great applause getter in the musical format. Of course many of the new multi-purpose theatre spaces are not equipped with curtains and require blacked out lights and drilled stagehands who also became part of the show.

Expressionism with its view of the machine age allowed stage mechanics to expose their machinery. Also their emphasis on robots and the soullessness of modern man influenced futuristic costuming and makeup and the use of new plastics and artificial materials on the stage. Unlike the realistic theatre costumes could have exposed zippers and be changed in view of the audience when desired.

Acting style in a predominately realistic age was harder to reconcile to the non-realistic plays, however. Vsevelod Meyerhold, a Russian compatriot of Stanislavsky developed an opposing system of his own which he called bio-mechanics. A series of gymnastic exercises which substitutes physical exercise for emotional recall as a method of bringing forth the inner truth of a characterization. This highly presentational style also demanded a new kind of scenery which was merely a machine on which to perform. This scenic style, known as **Constructivism**, like the gymnastic acting style was soon adapted to the more avant garde theatre forms which espoused a presentational approach.

Theatrical Fragmentation

The twentieth century saw more diversity of theatrical form than any of the previous ones in our study. Diverse and innovative approaches have almost become the intended end of many modern productions. This fragmentation grew out of a variety of impulses in society as well as the arts.

The first realist plays faced difficulty in finding an acting company willing to produce them. The nineteenth century was a time of great national houses which held monopolistic license and of direct and powerful government censorship. Ibsen's realistic drama **Ghosts** with its interlaced themes of venereal disease, incest and euthanasia became a case in point. Though sales of the printed copies showed the presence of potential audiences, critical and political response made productions in the traditional manner out of the question. Into the vacuum stepped Antoine with his Theatre Libre. The concept was to run a theatre by subscription. Since the audience was made up of members of a private organization, public censorship laws could not apply. Soon small "independent" theatres opened all over Europe, among which we've already mentioned: the Moscow Art Theatre which still produces today.

These independent theatres set a number of precedents and opened a variety of possibilities. Since they only played to a small house it became possible for single plays to be aimed at particular, if limited, groups. Theatre did not have to please everyone at large. This allowed splinter audience sensibilities to support their own artistic views and still make a profit. It allowed actors to develop the skills required of a certain style rather than training in the broad generalized "national theatre" styles prevalent in the nineteenth century. Modern cities today all include a variety of small venues each specializing in its own ethnic or artistic style and selecting its repertory accordingly.

Technical Needs of Independent Theatre

As these independent companies and their individual styles developed they brought into prominence several individuals whose skills would come to great prominence in the twentieth century. First among these was the modern director.

Modern Directors

As we already know an individual outside the stage picture was needed when pictoral style began to predominate. In addition the breakdown and scattering of repertory houses meant that actors could no longer pass on their "lines of business" or traditional role interpretation and therefore a coach to realize these essential elements was needed. The director as we now call him filled both needs.

Acknowledged founder of this new combination of skills was George II, Duke of Saxe-Meinningen. On his estate he turned a former opera house into a venue for his own theatrical productions. Primarily an artist, he first did sketches of the main scenes of each play and then substituted his own servants and hired actors to bring these pictures to life. He could spend lavishly on background and costume design and could afford long rehearsal periods to gain ensemble effect which he drilled into even the smallest detail of crowd scenes. His production methods and their results spread throughout the theatre world and soon he was a source of universal duplication.

Two other major director-theorists have already been named: Stanislavsky and Meyerhold. In addition to theses two Russians the German Max Reinhardt deserves mention for his stalwart development of the **Eclectic** style. Where most companies and theorists sought to propagate an individual style which they could impose on all the plays they produced, Reinhardt theorized instead on the style for which each single play had been written and sought to duplicate it. Shakespeare's plays then, rather than being staged in a constructivist jungle gym, a symbolist forest of vague scrims and projections, or even in modern dress with motorcycles and machines guns, was presented in Elizabethan tights and neck ruffs on a replica of Shakespeare's own Globe Theatre. He also staged Greek tragedy in an athletic arena and a Medieval morality play on the front steps of a great Gothic cathedral.

Modern Designers

Of course the other individual whose talents became indispensable in the new theatre ventures was the designer. Most came forward as an embodiment of the theories of the German opera composer, Richard Wagner. Wagner had argued for a fusion of all of the arts in theatre under the master control of one superior artist. In addition to his advocacy of a unified production he is credited with many performance innovations which twentieth century theatre construction and practice have continued. His theatre at Bayreuth included a concealed orchestra pit and a system of house lights that could allow the audience to sit in a dark "aesthetic distance." The auditorium had no center aisle or side boxes in what has now come to be known as "Continental seating."

Two designer theorists are remembered for developing these Wagnerian theatrical theories into their modern acceptance: Adolphe Appia and Gordon Craig. Appia insisted on three dimensional scenery as an environment for the three dimensional actor. He also developed modern stage lighting techniques to sculpt the actor and scenery rather than merely as illumination. Craig denied the existence of subsidiary artists and believed there could only be one master artist dominating every aspect of the production. Eventually this helped promote the director to his present position of authority.

All of which brings us to our present day. A time of great variety in styles, forms, scripts, and individual methods of production. These methods are a study in themselves. So it is to them we next turn our attention.

Identifying Modern Trends: Reading a Modern Play

Realistic Movement:
Realism

1. Strive to depict the real world through direct observation.
2. Visual elements of stage promoted accuracy of detail.
3. Realistic motivated dialogue and exposition.
4. All scenes causally related: leading to a logical outcome.
5. Dialogue, settings, costumes, business selected to reveal character.
6. Each role conceived as a personality formed by heredity and environment.
7. Each act of structure carefully rises to climactic curtain.
8. Theatre must be a source of insight, not just entertainment.
9. Usually three act prose.

Naturalism

1. Strives to depict real world through five senses.
2. Heredity and Environment must be scientifically laid out.
3. No right and wrong judgements; only facts.
4. No rigid structure for theatrical effect - slice of life staging.
5. Great emphasis on setting and props - usually not very glamorous ones.
6. Groups of people studied; no central character.
7. Dialogue copies random speech.
8. No such thing as a happy ending.
9. Developed long one-act play.

Anti-Realistic Movement:

Symbolism

1. Truth cannot be grasped by the five senses.
2. Truth cannot be expressed logically, we must grasp it intuitively.
3. Symbols evoke feelings and states of mind.
4. Universal truth is independent of time and place.
5. Great drama requires verbal beauty.
6. Sense of mysterious forces at work in human affairs.
7. Atmosphere of mystery must envelope the work.
8. Subject is the past or a fantasy world to lift us out of the hum-drum.
9. Interchangeable short scenes marked by pauses and silences.

Expressionism

1. The true world is only a distorted view through a personal eye.
2. The world is a threatening one.
3. Characters are not complete, only symbols.
4. One individual serves as our audience view.
5. Scenes are fragmentary and shift frequently.
6. Requires elaborate costume, scenery devices of the modern stage (lights - sound).
7. Machinery and Society have become dangers to man's existence.
8. Ambiguous and unclear solution; no clean cut denouement.
9. Often a formal, cyclic form.

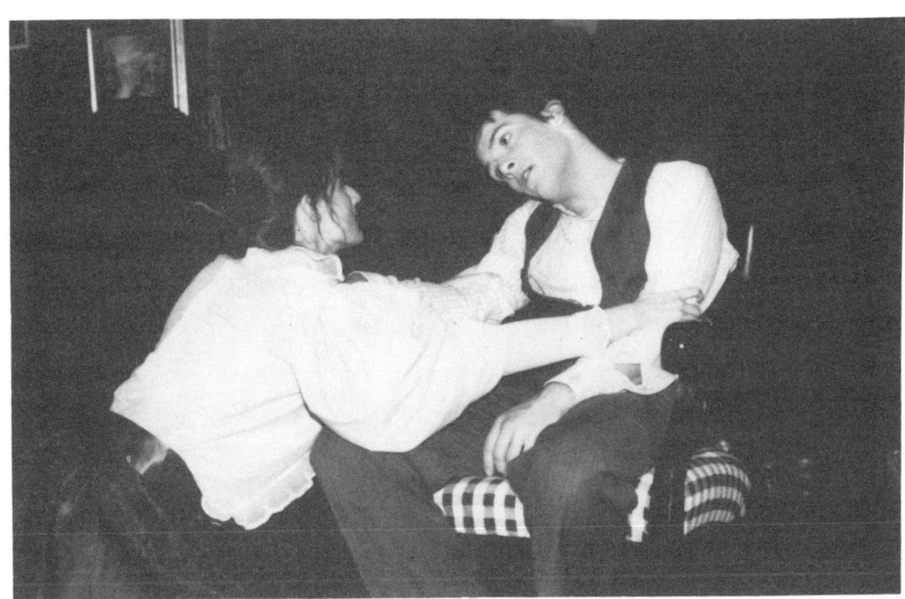

Realism: One of the great curtain scenes from all theatre, the final moment in Ibsen's **Ghosts**. Mrs. Alving comes to the realization that Oswald her son has suffered an irreversibly debilitating stroke and she must confront her promise to help him die by administering the morphine tablets he has hoarded for just this event. Through careful preparation the playwright has laid out all aspects of the argument but he leaves Mrs. Alving's decision dramatically up in the air at the curtain allowing each audience to go home debating the reasoning and morality of euthanasia and drawing its own conclusions. The depth of characterization and the universality of theme have kept the play as timeless and gripping as when it was written.

Anti-realism: In **The Seagull** by Chekhov, the young poet Konstantin stages a play he has written in the new avant-garde style for his mother who is a dramatic actress of the old school. This play within a play thus allows for satire of the new anti-realistic trends. In this production staged in the round the director has also made use of experimental artistic trends of the time which were much influenced by the theatre of the Oriental. The figure center represents "the universal world soul" centuries after all life has perished from the earth, the stagehands are in the Oriental manner, invisible. "Decadent!" declares the older actress, as she stops the show.

UNIT III

Contemporary Theatrical Production: Aims and Methodology
How does the play come about?

"Well, then what are we waiting for? Hit it!"
Sganarelle's Scandal by Torp and Spineti

Chapter Twelve
The Originators

The Three Approaches

Our historical studies have shown us the importance of understanding contemporary theatrical production practices in order to come to a full understanding of the plays of any given era. Along with the philosophical views accepted by an age and the stylistic aims of the individual playwrights, the production of the play is the primary critical experience where any audience is concerned. We judge the theatre even as we experience it. And the experiencing of it in this modern age is more than ever in the hands of a production staff. So if we as students intend to temper our critical reaction with knowledge of the "where for" and "how to" and to widen the range of our theatre-going experience, we need to look at contemporary production methods and means. As our historical units also showed us, this must begin with an understanding of the aims at the base of these productions. In the twentieth century three major approaches predominate. For purposes of this study let us label these three: **Professional**, **Educational**, and **Community**.

Differences between the Three

There is of course a tendency for all three to overlap at the margins. Professionals can be detected in each of the other types, but when they work there they must adjust to the differing job discipline and hierarchy. The fundamental aim of the theatre group works a clear difference in some instances, as we shall see. Sometimes this difference is a subtle one. Always, however, the purpose for each individual member of the production team remains constant. It is the methodology that varies. And the power instilled in each individual. As you study the following, then, try to keep the three types clear in your mind. This will help you see how the play was affected, and guide you in a clearer understanding of a correct critical response to it.

Start by making a list of the types of theatre in your area. Begin with the Professional because they are the most prominent. They advertise the most, are featured most on TV and radio and book and magazine sales. And why not? Their aim is to make money! They spend money to keep their products before the public.

Professional companies are of many forms in this century. First of course are the Broadway and Off-Broadway productions. Their touring companies (sometimes called "The National Company," or the more lowly bus and truck shows) come next and play local auditoriums or road professional houses like New Haven's Schubert or Hartford's Bushnell Auditorium. After World War II, resident professional companies were formed following the example of the Guthrie Theatre in Minneapolis. Most major cities have one, the Hartford Stage Company is an example, and though they advertise that they are "not for profit" they nonetheless are professional in aim and money is their bottom line. Some professional local companies have specific types of theatre to sell, like the Goodspeed Opera House, which revives musicals and also keeps a second theatre busy developing new musicals which they hope to send to Broadway and more profits. There are also the dinner theatres. This craze seems to have peaked, however, and many professional houses closed leaving the community theatres to use dinner theatre nights as fund raisers. Finally include the so-called "straw hat" summer theatres that book a professional season during the summer months or the large tent houses that alternate touring musicals with rock stars and comics on tour in summer.

Educational theatres are more easily identified by the general public. Your high school, college, or university productions are educational in aim. They may be utilized to raise funds, but they are at the root an educational venture not only for the people putting them on, but also their audiences. The name, however, can fool you. The Yale Repertory Theatre is not an educational theatre, but a professional regional company.

Community theatres organize for recreational reasons. "Let's get together and put on a show for the fun of it" was their initial impetus. Though some of their personnel may be professionals, though they too may be fund raisers, they are recreational in aim. So check your community theatre group in this, your Gilbert and Sullivan society, your chorale that stages shows, your church's Passion Play. Also in this group are the summer recreation programs that stage musicals or plays in the town park, town hall or school auditorium.

Individuals assigned roles in the production of modern plays and musicals share common titles in all three types of theatre. We will see in the ensuing paragraphs how their functions fit into the production schedule and try to keep clear how the aim of the group can vary working procedures for each member of the production team. First let us define some concerns that relate to all forms of theatre.

Initial Terminology of Production

The **season** is a term that has effect on professional, educational and community theatre alike. It begins in the fall and ends in the spring like a school year. And it sometimes has a summer or hiatus season as well. In the professional theatre the aim is to open in the fall in order to get a good run by awards week in the spring and coast through the summer. Professional regional companies present a series of plays opening in the fall and concluding in the spring. Community theatres do the same. As do most educational groups. As we shall see this has an effect on many phases of production.

Also of consideration here is the number of plays to be presented and the manner of presentation: **stock** or **repertory**. Broadway professionals are concerned with only one play at a time. Regional companies, however, and community and educational venues present a number of plays in a season. When each play in the group is mounted and presented individually and then the next, and then the next, this is called stock production. When, however, as in Shakespare's day, a number of plays are rotated nightly this is called repertory production. This last has almost disappeared in this day of long run success but is still seen in England and on the Continent.

Then every form of theatre must concern itself with **royalties**. Royalties are the monies paid to the playwright for permission to perform his work. All theatres pay royalties: professional, educational, and community, there are no exceptions to the copyright law. Any play copyrighted is protected for 28 years, renewable once. That is if your nation signed the International agreement. The USSR did not! Older plays are protected only in newer versions, adaptations or translations. Check the cover page of the plays you are reading and you will see a royalty statement. Check the program of the play you attend and you will find one also unless it is a pirated production.

Older plays then do not require royalties. New ones cost more, also musicals cost much, much more. Several reasons here: first, there is a team to be paid not just one author; second they bring in more money so you must pay more to do them. Royalties are handled by agencies who contract the producer, supply materials (scripts, scores, sometimes even posters) and police the results through a clipping service that reads all local papers and reports back.

"This play presented by permission of Samuel French, Inc." is perhaps the most common line in any program. This company licenses most English and American playwrights' works. Other major play royalty agencies are: Dramatists Play Service, Dramatic Publishing, and Bakers Plays. Musicals were traditionally handled by separate companies, Tams-Witmark, and Music Theatre International, were the major two until Rodgers and Hammerstein formed a company to market their own highly successful products. And now Samuel French has also moved in to the field of musical as well as play publishing and marketing. The popular English composer Andrew Lloyd-Webber has incorporated himself for greater control over production and profit of his own works.

The Organization

Where Does it Begin?

It would be overly optimistic to say the whole process begins with the playwright's script. That he simply writes it, hands it to an agent who sells it to a producing company or one of the above named agencies and then sits back and collects his royalties. Hardly this simple! Many professional plays are commissioned by a producer and only after production made available to others. Educational theatres stage originals written by students for degree credit or by faculty as vanity productions to display student talent. Community theatres sometimes have a board member who is an amateur writer. Otherwise they tend to stick to tried Broadway popular fare. To reach a better understanding of how modern plays come about we need to look into the function of the first major individual in the production hierarchy: the **Producer**, and examine more closely the selection process each theatre goes through. It is in the selection that the process originates.

The Producer

The function of the producer in the modern theatre is most often confused with that other name that looms large in the production process: the director. Where the director is concerned with artistic aspects of the play, the producer's concerns are financial. This does not mean he cannot have effect on the artistic product, however. In the professional theatre where his power is all encompassing he has tremendous influence over the artistic results as we shall see. However, it is important that we evaluate his functions first from the financial outlook which is his primary purpose.

Producer's names are the top line in most posters, programs, and ads. From the professional theatre we see: "Florenz Ziegfield presents:," or more recently David Merrick, Rodgers and Hammerstein or Walt Disney Productions present:. In educational theatre we read: the Junior Class or the Thespian Society, or the Department of Theatre presents. Just as in community theatre the top line states the New Britain Repertory Theatre or the Windsor Jesters present. Note that in the professional theatre it is usually an individual name, not a group. This is a reflection of the power he holds over the final product.

The producer's functions in keeping with his financial purpose are to license the playwright's script; hire or supervise hiring of staff, production team, and cast; supply rehearsal and performance space; advertise and supervise ticket sales; raise necessary funding and its outlay; pay expenses and, of course, collect profits.

The professional producer usually only works on one production at a time. And he usually is responsible for the original impulse. Reasoning as follows: What will sell this year? Perhaps it is the Olympics, or election year? What show can be revived or rewritten? What popular novel or TV series can be reshaped to the stage? What big time star performer can be marketed to the so called "legitimate" theatre crowd? When the decision is made the efforts of this producer are zeroed in on the profit line. All decisions then stem from this aim: to make money. And interestingly it is not his own money he uses to finance the production. The professional producer begins as a money raiser. He solicits what are called **Angels**, individuals or corporations who invest money expecting a return percentage of profits should there be any. The producer of course gets his cut even if the show does not bring a profit. If one of the Angels demands his mistress or daughter be in the cast, the producer considers the money angle. He has full authority over casting as long as he meets union requirements. If a star performer is his trump card, that performer may make demands (Re-write that scene! Give me that applause song! Fire that chorus girl!) which he allows. Rarely is the writer's product held sacred. Tennessee Williams had to write new endings for his Broadway producers, the originals were too "artsy" and "gloomy" for a theatre going public to pay good money for. The professional producer can advertise however he sees fit. He decides whose names appear above the title of the play.

The major difference when he works in a regional professional house is first of all his title. He is called a **Managing Director** and his theatre is credited as Producer. Don't confuse Managing Director with Artistic Director even though he usually functions under this title also. It is under the title of Managing Director that he fulfills his producer's role. Regional houses usually have a business manager and sometimes a treasurer, and of course a publicity manager to carry out individual tasks, but the Managing Director's authority invested in him by contract with the theatre's governing board gives him the power of decision making. The other obvious difference is that he must select more than one play to work on each season. These must be laid out with the local market in mind. Open with a crowd pleaser in the Fall, close with a show that will sell season tickets for the coming year. Sprinkle with original plays with local concerns (inner city race relations; AIDS; state history) and plays that will generate government grants.

As you can see the professional theatre is still a major generator of original plays and musicals, even though revivals have become a Broadway standard lately. Still the profit made by the original producer is and continues to be a staggering sum. Yet as you can see the very commercial demands of this profit view have a great deal to do with the resulting plays. And remember that almost all community and a great deal of educational productions are not original but warmed over from the Broadway original. The professional producers still set the standard and though results may be artistic, this is not their goal. The goal of the professional producer is profit.

The educational producer may be your class treasurer or he may be called a business manager. As such he has little to say about the production process except for the budget. Usually staff are already under contract, cast are students. The play selection may be his concern only so far as signing royalty contracts. He generally does not have to rent rehearsal or performance space as almost all professional producers (again except regional houses) and many community producers do. Angels are not needed when the school generated budget is utilized. Profits if there are any may go back into the school's general fund or used for a year end party. Departments of drama or theatre may have a faculty member designated as Managing Director but he has none of the professional producer's authority and power. As such, however, he is a member of the production team for each show and therefore has a vote in selection. This vote however is usually tempered in terms of projected costs, available funds, and foreseeable student audience. Educational theatre with its emphasis on educating presents a large percentage of historical works which they deem of value. This is sprinkled with current professional shows of an experimental nature and originals by students. Rarely musicals, if and when a music department can be involved also.

Community theatres are usually always operated under an elected board of directors. From this group a producer is selected for each show which is part of the season. His authority then is no more than a normal board member and usually restricts itself as in the case of his educational counterpart to budget, royalties, advertising and ticket sales. Some community groups own a small facility whose rent or mortgage must be met regularly. Most of them, however, utilize town or local school theatres for which they pay a small fee per production. Some are granted space free of charge by local industries as a tax write-off. Though they do not solicit Angels as a practice many give blocks of tickets to charity groups which are underwritten by individual or local businesses. None of these concerns have effect on the product result. The community group does what it feels its public will enjoy. Warmed over Broadway hits, revivals of classic popular hits (rarely Shakespeare) and of course, musicals.

The Director

The function of the modern director, or as he is sometimes called: the Artistic Director, is primarily interpretive. That is, his purpose is to interpret the playwright's script for a particular audience. His means of interpretation are of course limited to the words of the script and the stage pictures he can illustrate them with. How he is allowed to arrive at these determine the power he has over these results. Again we must study each of our three forms to understand this factor.

The director with the least control over the interpretive results is the professional director. This is due to the fact that he is usually hired after most major decisions affecting his interpretation have already been decided by the producer or managing director. The play has been selected, most of the cast hired, as are the designers, and even the style may have been set. Though he has a choice before signing a contract he knows he is being chosen as is a professional football coach, for his track record. He is also usually expected to specialize: classical comedies, experimental plays, musical revivals, etc. Some directors tour around re-producing the same show for various professional houses. He may also be married to a big star and so be hired as part of a package deal. At any rate his interpretive means are already limited at his hiring.

The same is basically true in community theatre although there directors usually bid for spots after the board, with the help of a reading committee, has selected a season. They will be selected not necessarily for their expertise, training methods or disciplinary habits; but for their ability to make the largely recreational show a pleasant and "professional looking" event for both cast and audience. Like the professional director, the community artistic director can be replaced at any point in rehearsal if the board feels results are not forthcoming.

It is the educational director who has the widest range of power in his production and therefore can be most praised or faulted for the interpretive results. First of all it is he or she who selects the play. This allows him to make his or her own evaluation of season, prospective audience, talent pool, theatre to be used and at the same time his own enthusiasms and strong points. That puts him one step ahead of the other directors who aren't allowed the luxury of this advanced analysis of the script. Of course the selection in educational theatre is usually subject to a vote by other members of the production team who are also faculty. But the initial impetus for the choice is the director's own.

Secondly the director in educational theatre does his own casting. This is a major factor in interpretation. Any given role in a play changes dramatically in the hands of different actors. Rehearsal costuming, rewriting the script cannot alter individual human characteristics that each actor brings to every role he plays. Professional directors have their casts handed to them. Even regional theatres use what is called a casting director situated in New York City who puts together a package and signs contracts and sends the results out to the Artistic Director in Houston or Minneapolis. Community theatres usually cast with a casting subcommittee who advise the director on his choices.

Since the stage picture is equally important with these other concerns, the director's ability to work with his designers and get results is paramount. In educational theatre the design team is usually made up of colleagues of the director who thus has opportunity to know their working methods and abilities. Frequently the designers are students working out advanced projects. If so the director will have been involved in their selection for his show and may even have trained them earlier. Also in educational theatre it is usually the director who determines the style the production will take. As we already noted the professional director's designers are hired separately. Though he is expected to work with them they may be total strangers to his methods and views on the play at hand. Sometimes they are selected because they are artists of fame and may have no knowledge of theatrical needs and production discipline. Community theatres usually take their designs directly from the play scripts they purchase and the director is not involved.

We are most familiar with the director's responsibilities during the rehearsal process. Here the educational director is also given the widest leeway. In fact, he is usually selected and hired for the position and holds it only because of his background study in a wide range of methods, not like his professional peer who is hired by a producer selecting methodology suited to this one project. Educational rehearsals then may utilize Stanislavsky-oriented actor coaching for a modern realistic play and the same director may train biomechanic skills into his young cast for a play with a more avant-garde style in mind. Educational directors tend to be eclectic.

They also tend to do their own background research. The professional director usually works with an individual called a **Dramaturg**. This person's task is to research the play, study its origin, compare translations where necessary or musical transcriptions where they apply, and advise the director and producer. Most educational directors serve as their own dramaturgs. They also tend to cover special skills. A professional production finds a voice coach, fencing or fight master, and choreographer for dance already on the production team when the director arrives. Educators have to be their own, or seek compatible ones among their colleagues or students. Because he is his own authority in these matters his powers of interpretation are much enhanced over the professional who has little say in these choices.

During the rehearsal process the director is expected to block the show and plot out business for his actors. **Blocking** means laying out the movement pattern and **Business** is what an actor does with his body and properties. Here is where the professional director is allowed the widest freedom. Since he is working with a new play, often with the playwright present for rewrites, his creative interpretation ability can really be an influence at this stage. Movement and placement of actors determine much of what the audience comes to view as the real meaning behind the lines. Emphasis and subordination of actors within the stage picture are powerful tools. The educational director exercises the same freedom, but the community director usually takes his cues from the play scripts printed from the Broadway prompt books with blocking already marked in. Business is usually only refined in the professional and community venues. But in educational theatre where it is being taught to learning actors, the director again exercises a greater creative force.

Stage Areas and Related Vocabulary

During the blocking process actors and directors communicate with a basic vocabulary of stage areas and related body positions. We have already learned some of the vocabulary, but this is a good time to round out an understanding of it. Begin with stage areas: Upstage is away from the audience. Downstage is closer to audience. Left is the actor's left as he faces the audience. Right is his right. Center defines itself. Actors and directors abbreviate these terms when writing down blocking. Thus: SL is Stage left. URC designates up right center. Add an X and it means Cross up right center (XURC). Add a V and you have XURCV or cross up right center and sit. An inverted V means stand up.

Body positions relate to the actors facing toward or away from the audience. Thus **full front** and **full back** are obvious. So is profile left or right. 1/4 position is the most common position in realistic theatre because it looks natural on a stage whose walls are opened out at an angle. This position places the actor halfway between profile and full front. Two actors side by side in the same stage area are expected to stand 1/4 facing each other or "sharing" the scene. When one turns to focus on the other directly he is said to "give" the scene.

In all three forms of theatre the director is expected to serve as ideal audience, shaping and honing performances, voices, dramatic moments, pacing of scenes to what his audience will see and hear. In the end he also must see the process of coordination of all phases of the production through to opening night. Here all three directors operate more or less under the same process. However, once the show opens only the educational director stays on hand. Professional theatre directors are relieved of responsibilities as the show is frozen and turned over to the stage manager to run. So also in community theatre. Educational directors however are expected often even to give complete notes and continue to make changes and improvements right through the run. One of the basic tools utilized by many modern directors is called a **French Scene Plot Chart** (See Figure in Appendix) A scene by scene break down of the play it illustrates actors on and off stage and the meaning given by the director to each scene. He also can mark the MDQ on this.

The Actor

Because he is the most visible member of the production, the actor often receives the most credit or blame for the resulting play. He or she did not select himself for the role, nor cast the others who will show him up or off. He did not decide what to wear and how expensive it might be. He did not design his makeup or in some cases even apply it. He did not plan his own movements or business and the props he must use were handed to him. He did not determine rehearsal time and performance schedule. And he is dependent on others to inform him if he is too loud, not clearly seen, or too emotional in comparison to others in the scene. He does not even plan his own curtain call and final bow.

Yet his voice and body are the major tools of interpretation of the playwright's story. Theatres are built to allow accoustic and sight line support to him. He becomes the standard of scale against which sets and costumes are designed. The stage is a platform for his display. The director's skill is judged on the basis of his ability to work with actors.

The modern actor spends a majority of his time looking for his next job. Tryouts and callbacks are a constant concern. Even the longest running show closes or the actor outgrows the role. Even actors in a repertory company face yearly contract renewal.

Professional actors belong to the union called **Actor's Equity**. You must be a member of Equity to act in a professional company. (There are some exceptions made in regional companies as we shall see.) And you must be a union member to even try out. How then do new Equity members come about? They may be members of the Screen Actors Guild (SAG) or the easier to get into union for radio and TV performers (AFTRA) and simply transfer membership. Or they may work in regional houses in the apprentice roles allotted to non-union members for which they can accumulate points toward membership. Or they may get cast out of the regulation non-union "cattle call" tryouts. However they arrive at it, professional actors depend on their union status to assist them getting roles as well as in contract, salary, and insurance security matters.

Profesionals also depend on an agent to help them get work. The agents keep files of actors and notify them of upcoming casting opportunities. The actor supplies his own photos (head shots) and a brief list of roles he has performed. He is expected to make an appearance where needed (most casting is still handled in New York City) and prepare readings or improvise scenes. Since 75% of all working actors are in musicals he usually must be prepared to sing or dance and supply his own music, though a tryout pianist is on hand to play it.

Community theatres depend on newspapers and local publicity to bring in prospective performers. Equity actors are not allowed to perform with amateur groups. The group may also have some restrictions as to serving an apprenticeship within the group before becoming eligible, but otherwise tryouts are open. Educational theatre usually restricts tryouts and casting to enrolled students. For his reason educational actors find the widest range of parts open to them. Old age, youth, character, classic, comedy, tragedy: student actors are asked to try them all. Professional and community actors on the other hand are usually narrowly type cast in categories: old-age character woman; male tough guy; innocent young girl; style actor; dancer who can sing; lead singer; romantic lead; comic secondary; and on and on.

Once the actor is cast the rehearsal period begins. Now he is under the discipline of the director. The professional actor of course has his schedule policed by Equity, but it is the director and his assistant or the already appointed stage manager who regulate rehearsal The actors tasks now are role analysis for which all actors are dependent on the director and his interpretation. He must adjust his vision to that of the director or the production is flawed from the outset. Analysis helps the actor work out the blocking, line delivery, and business which make up the physicalization of the role. In the professional and community theatres actors are assumed to have been cast because they already have mastered these intricacies. Therefore the director of these actors usually consults them with his interpretation and allows them to demonstrate their skills from which he selects and sharpens the role projection he is seeking. In educational theatre however the director often resorts to "imitate me" methods.

As we have already seen in our discussion of the director, it is the actor's responsibility to depend on the director as his future audience. Projection of voice and dramatic meaning can only be judged by someone "out front" and this is part of the director's role in rehearsal. Then the actor must master the physical demands of the role: business, movement, fight scenes, dances. And most mysterious of all, but absolutely essential, he must master **memorization**.

"How did you learn all those lines?" is a question all actors hear. Each, I'm sure, has his or her own secret answer; but it remains a highly individual skill.

Unlike the director, actors must of course maintain the run of the show. Professional actors have understudies who rehearse regularly. Or they may be called in during a long run by the stage manager to sharpen up business or re-learn some music or dialogue. This also happens in community theatre with long runs. But most educational shows have such brief performance dates that this is unnecessary.

Though the lead actors or those playing multiple roles may have dressers to assist them, all actors are expected to put on and take off their own costumes and makeup. They also are responsible for picking up their property guns, messages, etc, from the backstage prop table and also to get these props back into the hands of the prop master or his crew. Professionals are compensated for extreme hair style changes, dying or altering of beards, etc.

So as we can see the modern actor in his visible role as storyteller must depend on those who originate the production idea, who assemble the production team, who cast and rehearse him. He also benefits from a behind the scenes production staff of equal importance. We will discuss them in the next chapters.

Both presentational and representational makeup are required for **Stumblebum: He Who Gets Slapped**, a musical by Torp and Spineti based on the Andreyev tragedy. Since the play is about clowns in a circus who wear makeup on the job however, all elements are in a sense representational. Research here involved studying European clown makeup to suit the locale of the musical.

Chapter Thirteen

The Designers and Artistic Staff

In the modern theatre, where style in its many manifestations has become so important, the designers have risen to a new position of prominence. They share a specialized working procedure and vocabulary.

First among these are the **scenic designer** and the **costume designer**. The scenic designer works closely with the **technical director**, who is usually responsible for constructing the designs into the stage setting. He is usually responsible for the design of all stage **props** or **properties**. These props may be weapons, furniture, even dishes and food, in fact any objects handled and used by actors as part of their business. Props may be designated as all set dressing as well, even though pictures and tapestries and chandeliers are not handled by actors. Some properties which are part of costuming (fans, gloves, eyeglasses) will be the costumer's design, and they all end up in the **properties manager**'s responsibility during production.

Both costume and set designers utilize what are known as the Principles and Elements of Design. There are five of each and they are standard terminology in all of the visual arts.

The **Principles of Design** are: Harmony, Balance, Proportion, Emphasis, Rhythm.

Harmony dictates a sense of things going together or in conflict. As so scenery and costumes can express the inner meaning of a staged scene. **Balance** indicates a presence or lack of stability and usually is expressed by symmetrical or asymmetrical forms. **Proportion** in theatre is always gauged on the scale of the human actor; his costume or the set can make him appear to be a giant or a midget. **Emphasis** allows the designers to point out a center of interest on the actor or the stage. **Rhythm** in design is a repeated element that leads the eye of the beholder in a certain direction.

The **Elements of Design** are: Line, Mass, Color, Texture, Ornament.

Line at its most obvious is straight or curved. Straight is serious, curved humorous. **Mass** refers to shape and space and again refers backs to a human sense of proportion. **Color** has many aspects: hue, saturation, intensity. Its combinations can be used to express emotional status as well as invoking them in the audience. **Texture** is the most clearly differentiated between costumes and scenery. In the set design texture (brick walls, wallpaper, hedges, even a cloudy sky) is usually achieved by a flat painted surface. In costuming, on the contrary, real textures (fur, leather, wool) are used. **Ornaments** are those distinctive touches that are used to characterize the locale or the period in time.

Modern designers are often asked to work with or originate on their own a **Dramatic Metaphor** or symbolic visualization of what the director or they feel expresses the play's inner qualities or theme. Sometimes this is an element of the scenery called for in the script (a stove, a portrait, a grove of trees) which is blown up all out of proportion to the rest of the set. Or it may be a highly stylized unrealistic environment (the world of the play is a cage, or a junk yard). Sometimes it is color alone that sends this symbolic message or metaphor. Modern audiences have come to accept it as a part of the "concept" of the play even though it is obviously stylized and not realistic.

The Scenic Designer

The original purpose of the setting was to conceal backstage areas from audience view. Masking the wings and flies of the modern proscenium theatre is still an expected part of a modern set, but it serves two broad additional purposes. It must aid audience understanding of the play and also it can express a play's inner qualities.

Good scenic design helps the audience identify locale and period of the drama. Usually modern playwrights give lengthy descriptions of the scenery for each scene, but classical plays left this to the individual production. The director may have decided to alter the standard approach (for example Shakespeare in modern dress, or Moliere moved to the American West). Scenery is the first way this change can be impressed on the audience. Of course, costuming and language are other ways. The scenery is also expected to clarify on stage and offstage areas. Where do exits lead to? This can be made clearer by the actor using them but the design supplies our first sight clue.

Modern sets also give actors and directors a variety of acting areas: levels, platforms, stairs, and ramps for variety in stage grouping. Finally the setting aids our understanding of the character, socio-economic status and taste of the persons who inhabit it in the play.

One of the inner qualities of every play which the setting can express is simply mood. Is it a gloomy day or a happy event that will take place here? Of course the lighting designer must assist here. Whether the play is tragic or comic can sometimes effect the design. Then, too, the level of probability should be established in the audience's mind. Is this a fantasy? A real story? An absurd parody? The set can tell us this. Style, of course, is a strong consideration. Is the play expressionistic? Naturalistic? Finally, as we have seen, the design may utilize a symbolic metaphor.

The Designer's Considerations

In planning his setting the designer must take into account: theatre to be used, budget, schedule, requirements of the script, actor-oriented sight lines and acoustics, and of course safety.

Three Shapes of Theatre

Modern theatres are set up in three basic formats (See Figure 10). These are proscenium, thrust or open stage, and arena or theatre in the round. Most professional and community houses are of the **proscenium** kind as we have seen. And most modern plays are written for this type of house. Educational facilities built in the last half of the century tend to be flexible allowing seating and staging area to be varied to any format. These are usually termed "black box" or "experimental;" houses. The **thrust** or **open stage** set up allows audience on three sides of a staging area. This still gives a place for curtained off scenes but brings the actor out closer to most of his audience. Here scenic walls can only be on one side and furniture and floor surfaces become more important to the design. **Arena** or **theatre in the round** places the audience all around the acting space. No scenic walls can be used. No curtain, either. Lights and props become all important. Scenes must end and begin with a light blackout and scene shifting will be witnessed by the audience.

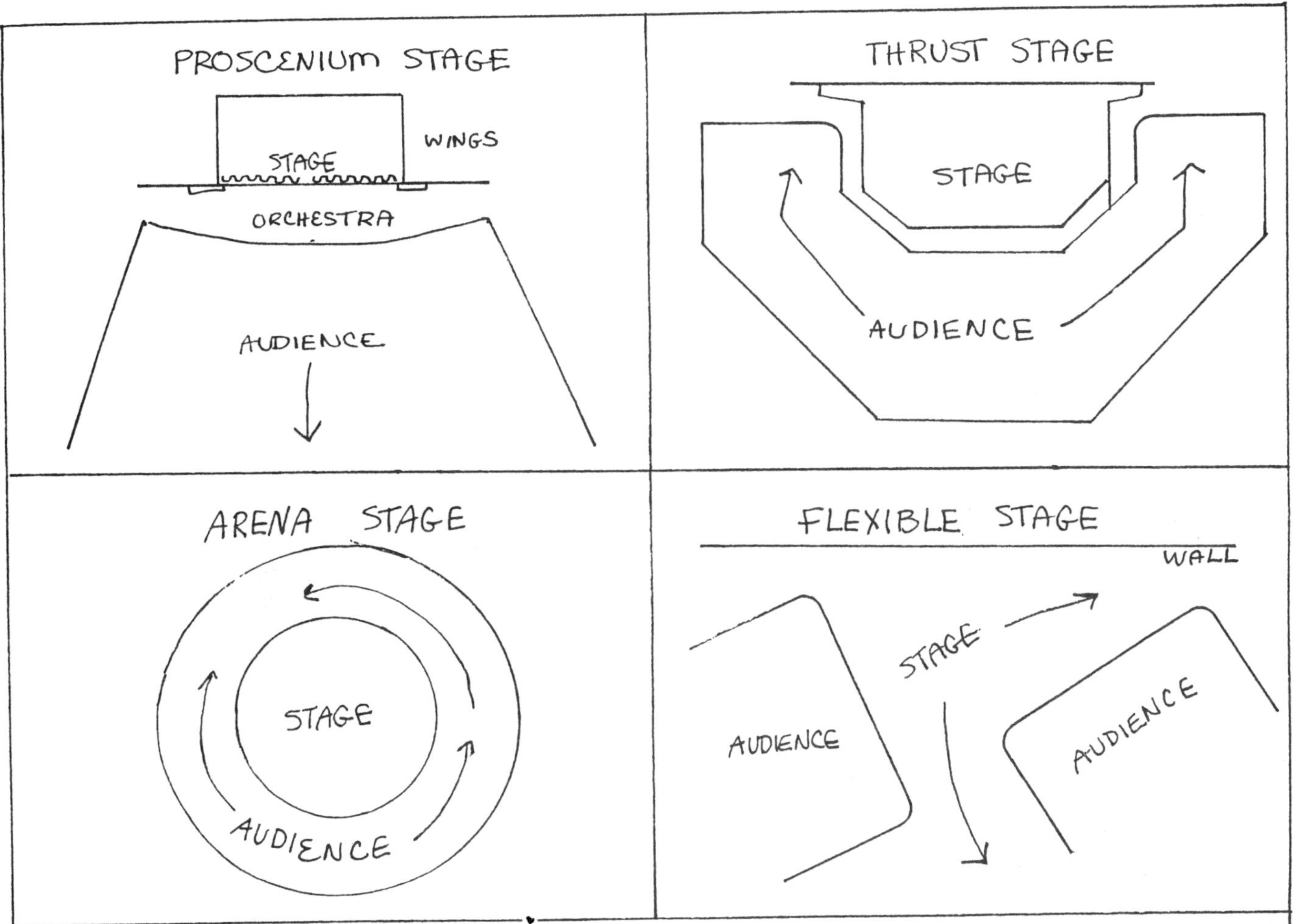

Budget and schedule of course vary. In the professional theatre every item of scenery must be budgeted new. Community and educational groups usually bring stock scenery and furniture out of storage and renovate them to the need of each show.

The standard unit of scenery in the modern theatre is called a **flat**. Flats are light wooden frames over which canvas or muslin have been stretched. They can be assembled into the walls of a box set, painted and decorated with door frames, pictures, often a ceiling piece, and give the appearance of a solidly built room. They can be taken apart, stored and repainted for further use. If a set must be shifted during performance they also are easy to move. As we have already seen, community and educational groups must have space to store and construct these; professional theatre only need to store what is used for one show at a time and they job construction from an outside source destroying the set at the end of the run. According to professional contracts the set cannot be reused, even in a touring show. A new set must be constructed for the tour.

The other standard scenic units are the stage **draperies**. These are free hanging curtains that are used in almost all proscenium houses, even your school auditorium, to mask offstage areas. Arranged like the old wing and drop sets, they consist of **legs** or **tormentors** along the sides masking the wings and **borders** or **teasers** across the top masking the flies. The front draw or drop curtain is sometimes called the **grand drape** and it and all other units of draperies must be fire-proofed. Standard color for draperies is black because this does not reflect light and therefore appears invisible to the audience. As a measure of economy, community and educational theatres sometime stage plays in a "drapery set". By this is meant the black masking drapes form the box set with window, door or fireplaces plugged in to suggest a complete room. Modern audiences seem to accept this convention even though the look is highly artificial. They also seem to accept the lack of a ceiling in a realistic box set. Professional houses, however, seldom resort to these money-saving devices unless the theatrical naivete is part of the dramatic metaphor intended.

Once the set designer knows the theatre space he will be using, his budget, and the schedule, he can proceed to the needs of the script. Does it require more than one setting? If so, a number of concerns come forward. Is there an act break or intermission between changes? Does the action return to their locale again? Sometimes the setting is constant but requires major redecorating to show time passage. Taking into account the kind of theatre being used, a shifting scheme must be decided. The director usually makes the decision.

Scenery can be "run" or slid on tracks or by stage hands into the wings if there is room. Or it may be "flown" into the flies if the theatre has a **counterweight** system or series of pulleys and rope tackle. Most professional theatres and some larger educational university houses have mechanical shifting devices such as rotating disks or revolving stage floors and elevator stage sections to raise and lower a complete box set. As you can see the choice of a theatre space can limit design features. The director may also decide to not use a curtain where possible in a proscenium house. This requires coordinated technicians of course, but must be planned from the design up. Many Broadway shows depend on the showy nature of revolving sets and flying chandeliers to get applause as the scenery shifts. Many realistic plays in thrust or arena theatres depend on a light curtain. This means a blackout during which black-clad stagehands madly race around making necessary changes.

Other considerations of the script are of course necessary entrances and exits. Hiding places, stairs, balconies, upper windows, or mountain passes may be mentioned in the script. Here the director again is consulted as to style. Sometimes he only wishes a suggested area like a constructivist set. Or he may wish to use a **unit set** where all locations are on stage from the outset and lights are used to shift from locale to locale. Projected scenery has also become a possibility with our new projecting devices. But this cannot work at all in an arena stage.

Style and metaphor are utilized by the designer also at the director's approval.

In all this of course the actor must be seen and heard by the audience. This is easiest to control in a proscenium house where down center prevails as a strong point and upstage areas can be elevated with platforms, etc. In arena design the designer is often limited to furniture and floor coverings.

Safety concerns are never out of mind. These, however, usually deal with construction methods and storage of shifted sets so as not to block exits. Exit lights not being covered can be critical in some black box houses.

The Design Process

With these considerations clarified, the designer's artistic and creative skills can be unleashed. If the play requires it, research into a foreign locale or time, a specific milieu, a rare background, is undertaken. What the set designer is required to produce first, however, is a floor plan. This layout of walls, entrances, and furniture on the prospective stage floor is required before the director can begin his blocking of the action. It will also aid the lighting designer in his first light plot planning.

Once the floor plan is decided on and approved, the designer either makes a model set or paints a series of front views of the scenery which are called **elevations**. These illustrate in scale what the set will look like. Sometimes even lighting effects are painted on and usually a human figure is added to show scale. The elevations or the model will of course be used by the technical director for construction and the set painter, but the director must approve them. More useful to the technical director are the designer's **working drawings**. These are views of the scenery from behind showing all construction features, which flats will be used, how braced, how joined, etc (See Figure in Appendix).

In the community and educational theatre stock scenery is of course referred to and only unique new pieces constructed. Here the designer is usually his own technical assistant even doing the painting or supervising it. In the professional theatre, however, union rules forbid the designer from touching the flats. He can only stand by and watch his elevations being transferred to the full scale stage set.

Dressing the set, or adding curtains, wall hangings, floor coverings, furniture, etc. comes next. This usually occurs only just before dress rehearsal. The set designer's task is figuratively completed once the show opens and no more changes are needed.

The Costume Designer

As we have already noted the costume designer shares many of the scenic designers concerns. The Elements, the Principles, Design Metaphor, these are terms familiar to this individual as well. The costume design also is utilized in the modern production to serve two purposes: to aid understanding and to express inner qualities.

Like scenery, the costumes in a play can identify period and establish locale. They also indicate time of day and even the occasion required for the action. Social and economic status, even occupation, are indicated by clothing and hairstyle. They also signal the age of the character to an audience.

Inner qualities of character may be subtly or broadly pointed up by the costuming. They help sort out character relationships. Sometimes this is a subtle use of color to tie together young lovers in our minds. Or it may be an obvious use of logos or family crests to separate opposite warring factions in a historical drama. Any of the elements may be utilized by the costumes to point out a character's importance in a scene. Of course costumes must unite intangible qualities like mood and style. Here they work closely with the set designer's concepts. Where the inner psychological state of the character is important the actor may find the costume designer an invaluable help. Sometimes the costuming is used to illustrate a progression the character undergoes: growing anger, maturing, weakening resolve, a progression of emotion to a climax.

The Designer's Considerations

In planning the costumes the designer must take into account: the actor and cast, the theatre to be used, budget, schedule, requirements of the script, progression of the show, comfort and safety.

Like the set designer the costume designer needs to take into account the theatre in which the play will be presented, particularly if an open or an arena set up is involved. These place the audience closer to the actor and allow him or her to be viewed from all sides, therefore requiring much more attention to detail and construction methods. (No visible zippers in period plays!) It is the actor and casting of the shows that is of primary concern where the costume design is concerned, however. Costume detail can cover a multiple of physical problems. And since the costumer's task is the total look of the actor: clothing, personal adornment, hair style, makeup, the designer must take into account the complete physical appearance of each actor cast, not merely clothing measurements. When a crowd scene or a chorus is involved the designer must know if the director wishes a massed uniform look or the more realistic approach where each individual is given distinguishing and unique characteristics. In either case he must look them all over before designs can be completed.

Budget and schedule concerns are the same as those of the scenic designer. Again the professional builds (or rather has built) new costumes which will go back to a rental house after the show. Community and educational designers work from stock items or may on occasion rent from rental houses such difficult and unusual items as armor, tuxedos, animal costumes. In this case the rental agency may make some alterations, but the costumer's designs are limited by what is available and how it can be altered or restyled.

Script concerns involve physical actions required of the actor. This of course is enhanced or altered by the director's blocking or in the case of a musical, the choreographer's dance requirements. As such, this concern delays part of the design process to a later point in the production schedule. Costume designers find themselves making changes for physical needs of the actor right up until opening night and sometimes after.

Not only must the costume fit and be comfortable and take wear and tear of performance, it sometimes must be changed quickly. Costume changes to show time passage, off stage events, or when one actor plays more than one role must be as smoothly planned as set shifting. These are not last minute concerns. The designer needs to know them early in the process. And of course the safety of the actor may require padding, concealed flying rigs and fire proofing. Sometimes a costume must be bloodied or soaked or torn every night. These "accidents" are also designed in advance.

As I have also indicated it is usually the costume designer who designs hair and makeup, and selects hand props that are part of a character's over-all look (fans, hats, gloves, handkerchiefs, pipes, canes, even weapons).

The Design Process

Research in costume design requires much more detailed study than that of the scenic designer. Where broad architectural styles such as Gothic, Rococo, or Federalist Revival can indicate an era in the scenery, fashion changes in costumes can pinpoint a country, and differentiate two close periods (the 1870's from the 1880's for example). It is in the costuming that the director most clearly re-sets a period production, especially on a thrust or arena stage.

The director also needs to confer with the designer concerning this information when, for example, hoop skirts will affect his blocking.

The designer begins with a series of costume sketches (See Figure in Appendix). When these are approved, fabrics and patterns can be considered. In the professional theatre this is turned over to a costume house whose seamstresses mock-up, fit, and keep in repair the designer's work. They also continue to own the clothes and accoutrements and reclaim them for rental purposes when the show closes. Some community or educational facilities employ or volunteer sewers, but often the designer is his or her own construction assistant.

As in the case of the set designer, the community and educational costumers must be adept at utilizing stock costumes. This makes the design process in these venues much more a re-design or re-invention process. This should not be regarded as a hindrance to creative design, however. The end product can be a delight of original and stylistically unified characters moving against an aesthetically pleasing background.

To assist in the run of a show the costumer may supply a **costume chart** and a **make-up plot**. These consist of a scene by scene, character by character breakdown of the play indicating costuming or makeup needs and changes for each. Like the director's **plot chart** and a set designer's **shifting scheme**, these charts go to the stage manager and his prompt book (See Appendix).

The Lighting Designer

Most often regarded as an adjunct of the scenic design, this individual has grown to prominence in the age of computer driven effects. Also the popularity of arena and thrust stages makes lighting a major concern. Lighting designers have fewer controllable factors than the other designers, however, and their contribution comes much later in the rehearsal schedule.

Light can only be varied according to brightness, color stage area and possible movement. Brightness, of course, depends on dimmers and power sources and usually is preset on computers. Color in lighting is achieved by using **gels** or colored transparencies mounted in front of the naked instruments. Cheaper than a whole series of colored bulbs and easier to store, these gels tend to fade and during a long run show, will need to be changed frequently. The moving light source or **follow spot** light usually always requires manual operators.

Theatre shape plays a major part in light design. Thrust and arena lighting requires particular skill and care of installation because the audience is close to and surrounds the acting area. Lights must beam on the actors without getting in the spectator's eyes.

Functions of Lighting Design

Lighting is used for several purposes. It must illuminate the setting and stage area. It should help the audience see the actor, especially facial expressions and sculpt his three dimensional nature. Then it can be used simply to tell the time of day and weather. Because of its emotional effect it can also be used to express inner meaning to scenes and to dramatize characters' feelings. It is often used to emphasize important characters in a scene or stage areas or props. All light sources are also part of the designer's task since real flame is only very rarely allowed in the theatre. Thus candles, fireplaces, torches, and oil lamps required by the play or the set design are electrically operated and made to appear to give off real light.

The Design Process

Once the designer of light has been given his budget, schedule, theatre and the concept (presentational exposed lights or representational realisitic sources), he or she, like the director, requires a floor plan. With this he can draw up a **light plot**. This is a master plan of the theatre showing placement of each instrument and which areas of the stage they will be focused on. Color and brightness will be set only after the instruments are in place and the setting as well. Color can be used to alter set and costume colors, so the lighting design in this concern can only follow the other designers.

Once the stage areas are mapped out the designer makes out a **cue sheet** for the director to approve. This is a master instrument plan moment by moment in the script wherever a change in lights is required. Eventually when the lights cues have been programmed onto a dimmer board or computer panel, the cue sheet is given to the stage manager and the light technicians who will run the show. During final rehearsals light cues are often adjusted during run-through rehearsals, but professional productions always require a **cue to cue** test of each light set up with just the technicians and director, no actors present.

Other individuals who are sometimes listed among the designers include sound designer and choreographer. The sound designer plans the musical and sound effect background when one is of sufficient sophistication to require an overall plan. Musicals, of course, require accompanists and music directors, but their "design" is usually established by the composer. Choreographers plan dance and movement patterns and are rarely used outside of musical production. The artistic nature of their contribution however marks them for inclusion under this heading.

The technical requirements for staging A. Strindberg's expressionistic **A Dream Play** are a stretch for the imagination and technical skill of any producing group. Here the scenic fluidity is achieved by moving stage platforms and multiple background projections on a transparent cyclorama.

Chapter Fourteen
"Techies" and the Production Schedule

"**Techies,**" as they are called, are the individuals of the technical staff supporting each production. Begin with those who hold the script prompting actors or calling cues, including those who set up and shift scenery or props, work lighting controls, balance sound volumes, repair and clean costumes, apply or remove makeup, and never forgetting of course the battalion of front of house personnel: ticket sellers, ushers, publicity agents.

Several among the group merit special definition and discussion before we begin to follow a modern production through its process of realization. There are also a few terms unique to theatrical practice which we will define.

We have already mentioned the individual called the **Technical Director** on the show's program. His function is to see to construction of the working drawings of the set designer. In educational theatre he usually functions as shop foreman or master carpenter and sees that stock scenery is put back in storage after a show closes. As such also tools and supply inventories are his responsibility.

Backstage Discipline

The key individual in production discipline from early in rehearsal through the run of a show is the **Stage Manager**. This individual has authority over all backstage and onstage personnel. He or she maintains the prompt book and thus all scripts changes, blocking diagrams, sound and light cues (including advanced warning for each), cast lists with appropriate telephone numbers. During rehearsal periods he is responsible for stage set-up, rehearsal furniture, taped-out floor plan, scripts, rehearsal props and costumes where needed. During the show's run he maintains a sign-in sheet, calls latecomers or supplies understudies, gives warning curtain time to the dressing rooms. It is the stage manager who signals the show's start and end. In the professional theatre the stage manager takes over the director's role after opening night. With the producer he sees to last minute substitutions if a cast member is sick. He rehearses scenes which he feels are getting sloppy. And he is required to hold understudy rehearsals in full costume and makeup once a week. In community and educational theatre his power may not be as all encompassing, but his authority is the same. Most stage managers come from the ranks of assistant directors. And most regard the job as training ground to become a full scale artistic director.

Under the stage manager's authority in direct chain of command are the Properties manager, or **Prop Master**, wardrobe and makeup supervisors, stage crew (professionals usually use the TV label **Grip** with their supervisor called the Key Grip). Light board operator, sound controller, and their assistants and crew members. Musicians, dancers, actors also come under his direct line of order during the performance.

Front of House

In front of the curtain and in the lobby areas the discipline is controlled by the **House Manager**. In community and educational theatre this is usually a pre-supposed part of the Managing Director's job. After all he must be present all through the run of a show to manage the ticket sales, so the running of the house seems natural. The house manager opens the box office, opens the house or auditorium, supervises ushers, maintains audience discipline, clears the house and sees to cleaning, seat repair, etc., counts returns and sees them deposited and locks up. Those are his responsibilities and his assistants are either volunteered or hired as the venue allows.

There is a careful shift of front of house discipline at show time. The stage manager controls the house and stage at first while props and lights and sound are checked one at a time. Sometimes also the actors, singers or dancers may warm up on stage before the audience is let in. When the stage manager feels the stage is ready he signals the house manager and turns the discipline of the house over to him. The head usher can open up the auditorium and let in the audience. Only when the house manager feels the audience is in and ready does he turns this authority back to the stage manager. He can delay if important people are expected or if there s a hang-up in the lobby. Only when he has re-assumed discipline can the stage manager signal the show to start. he may have delays of his own (cast members late, props out of place, lights being replaced) but he is the one who calls the start and stop: "Curtain!"

The stage manager also calls the **Strike**. Strike is another theatrical term that does not mean what it does beyond stage doors. Strike in the theatre means to take it down and put it away. There are two kinds. Every night of performance props and costumes no longer needed are "struck" by their respective crews. At the end of the performance some valuable furniture and set dressings may also be locked in a prop room or safe space. Then there is the final strike when the show closes. In the professional theatre the set is destroyed or sold in pieces. Costumes return to the rental house or in modern dress shows may be presented to the actors. In community and educational theatre things are returned to stock after being stripped of specific detail. It is the stage manager's task to call and supervise this strike.

One other term regarding the backstage functions of the modern theatre is worthy of mention before we begin the production process. This is the name given to the designated backstage area set aside for actors and techies to relax: the **Green Room**. No one knows for sure why it is called this, but all theatre people know it by the name. It may be used for informally assembling the cast and crew for announcements before a show or for "notes" afterwards.

The Production Schedule

1. Selection

It all begins here. The playwright must get someone to choose his play to produce. This is usually the producer although in educational theatre the director is most often the decider. Playwrights of course use agents. The decisions come about by consideration of season, budget, royalty contracts, availability of theatre, acting pool and suitability to the aims of the producing group.

2. Production Conference

Once the play is selected and contracted, a major conference is called. The producer calls it in the professional theatre, the board of directors in the community theatre, and the director in educational theatre. At this conference all members of the production team meet to confer. In the professional theatre there may be 75 people present. And this includes professional actors already signed. The production is discussed, members meet and learn each other's ideas and decisions are clarified. Budget, schedule, specific requirements of the script, design metaphor or concept and lines of authority are mapped out.

3. Casting

In professional theatre this may already be started, but it now must be completed. Tryouts are followed by call backs of specific people and then roles are assigned. During this period set designers proceed with floor plan. Costume designers research.

4. Rehearsal period

Directors work on coaching, blocking and eventually integration during run-throughs. Sets are designed and built. Also costumes. Props assembled. Lights are hung and focused. Sound and music rehearsed and recorded. Publicity and ticket sales set up. All of these elements will come together during the tech week or as it is affectionately dubbed: "Hell week."

5. Tech week

These events see the first assumptions of authority by the stage manager who begins to take over the run from the director. First come isolated technical events.

> 1. **Dress parade**: each costume is tried on and modelled for the director's approval. Movement required, lights utilized.
>
> 2. **Cue to cue**: lights, scenery shifting, sound cues all are tried out and timed usually without the cast, only the stage manager and necessary techies. When an actor has to signal a light cue from onstage he may be present to check it out. Only when this has been completed can a complete rehearsal be assembled.
>
> 3. **Tech rehearsal**: this is a start and stop affair run by the stage manager. Every cue in the production must be tried and set from curtian to curtain. Costume changes, set shifting, music cues and curtain calls must be drilled.
>
> 4. **Dress rehearsals**: these are necessary to establish the rhythm of the show. Now no stopping is allowed except in dire emergency. All conditions are show conditions but changes may still be made. In the

professional theatre tickets can be sold, but no critics may review until official opening night. Educational and community theatres usually invite audiences, especially for comedy and musical shows, to accustom their actors to their reactions. The stage manager is now in control although the director still gives notes and makes changes.

5. **Opening and the Run**: Now the production is "frozen" except in educational theatre. Critics review, directors and most rehearsal and design staff go on to their next job. Producer and actors continue the run. The stage manager is now in charge.

6. **Strike**: Equity requires one week's notice for the closing night. Though regional professional houses, community and educational theatres may extend a run, their closing night is usually set from the start of production.

The Critic

You will probably notice that I have not discussed critics as a part of production. This is because they are not members of the team. They are outsiders by the nature of their job which should require objective analysis with no conflict of interest. They are hired by the media: newspaper, magazine, TV or radio station. And their task is supposed to be to inform readers or listeners about what to expect from this production. They also should evaluate in terms of their specific readership the worth of attending this particular event. This requires a knowledge of the play's aims, background, purpose. It also assumes a responsibility to a particular public.

Critics tend to regard their job to be an opportunity to make clever puns and witty remarks about the play. They also seem too often to merely list what they regard to be wrong with the play without a sense of evaluating the responsibility behind the script and its interpreters. On the other side of the coin clever publicity agents tend to regard critics merely as a source for culling out advertising slogans.

The student of theatre should trust to his own instinct and learn to read these reviews in order to make his own decisions. Better still is the attitude of the student who attends the theatre because he likes to test his own knowledge and be his own critic.

So there it is, your abbreviated look at theatre. Whether you appreciate the art of it or admire its craftsmanship, it is there for all to enjoy. And enjoy it we have, for all these centuries. The next will be no exception.

Lorca's poetic tragedy **Blood Wedding** is here seen staged in front of a unit set whose three arches become a background for the otherwise disjointed impressionistic scenes. At the same time they serve as a metaphor for the three symbolic women of the plot: mother, bride, and wife. Fantasy scenes were staged behind the scrim-cyclorama. Note painting of the setting and sculpturing of actors achieved by lights. Live music and sound supplied by cast members.

APPENDIX

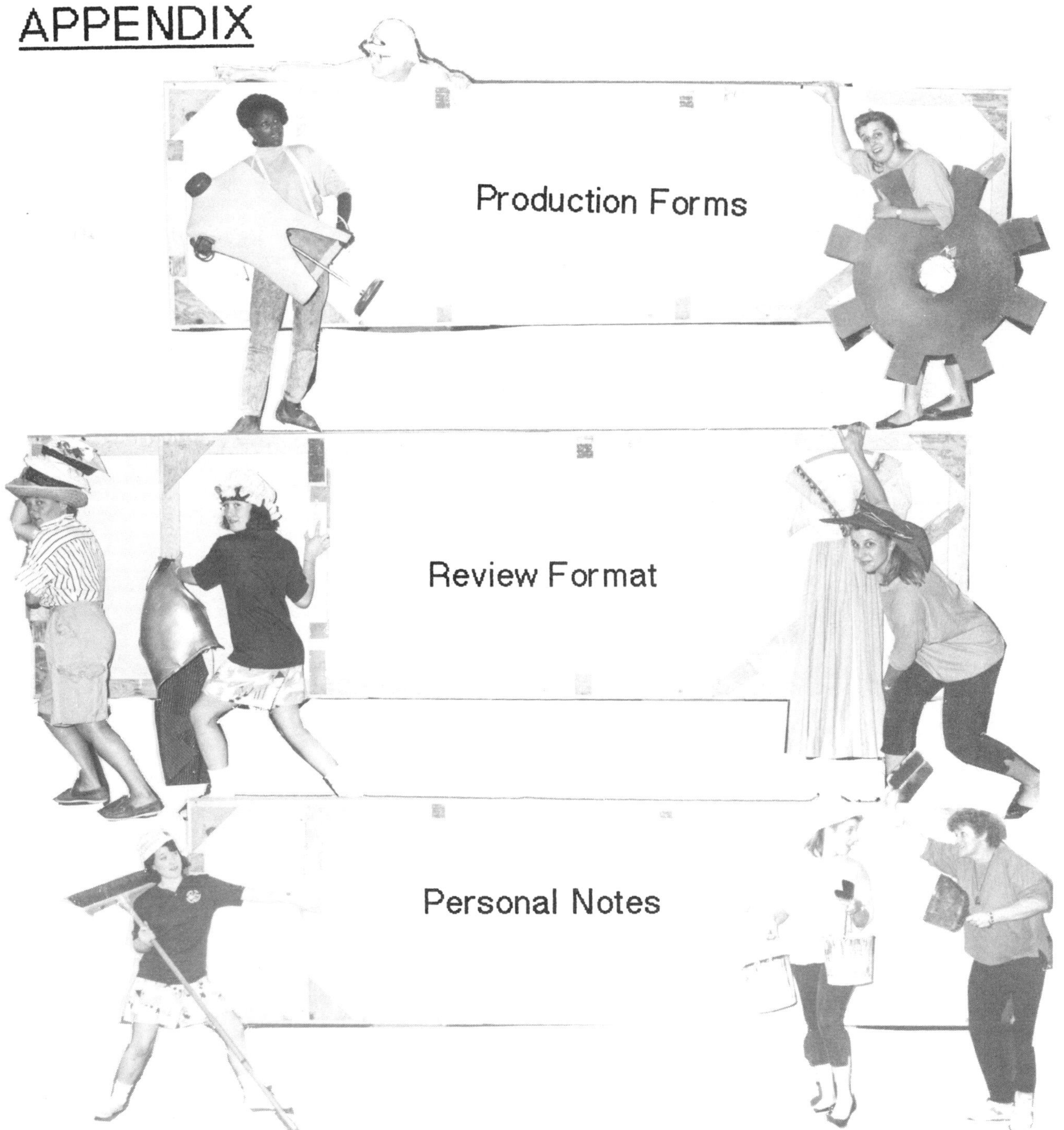

"If only we knew... if only we knew!"
Three Sisters by Anton Chekhov

FRENCH SCENE PLOT CHART

GHOSTS by. H. IBSEN

ACT	I										*						II
SCENE	1	2	3	4	5	6	7	8	9	10	11	12	13	14	15	16	
PAGES	20-27	27	27-28	28	28-30	30	30	30	30-39	39-45	45-53	53	53	53	53-54	54	
ENGSTRAND	X																
REGINA	X	O	X		X			O					X		O.V.		
PASTOR MANDERS			X	O	X	X	O	O	X	X	X	O	X	O	X		
MRS. ALVING							O	O	X	X	X	X	X	O	X		
OSWALD										X		X	X	X			
	Exposition: Rain; will R. go to town with E.	R. gets rid of E.; Prepares self for M.	More rain talk. Raincoats	M. and papers	Discuss going to town; R. makes play for M.	M. sees shocking books	Mrs. A. Enters	Sends R. out then can talk.	Discussion Relationships; orphanage; Insurance	Oswald + his father's pipe; Argument over life of artists.	* Confession: the real Capt. Alving exposed	Oswald returns	R. and O. set up dinner	O. follows R. off	"Ghosts" are heard off stage!	Empty stage – Slow Curtain	

X = on stage w/lines
O = on stage but silent
O.V. = off stage voice

* M.D.Q.:
Can Mrs. Alving purge herself of the "ghosts" by revealing the truth to her son?

ANYTHING GOES   Blocking Rehearsal

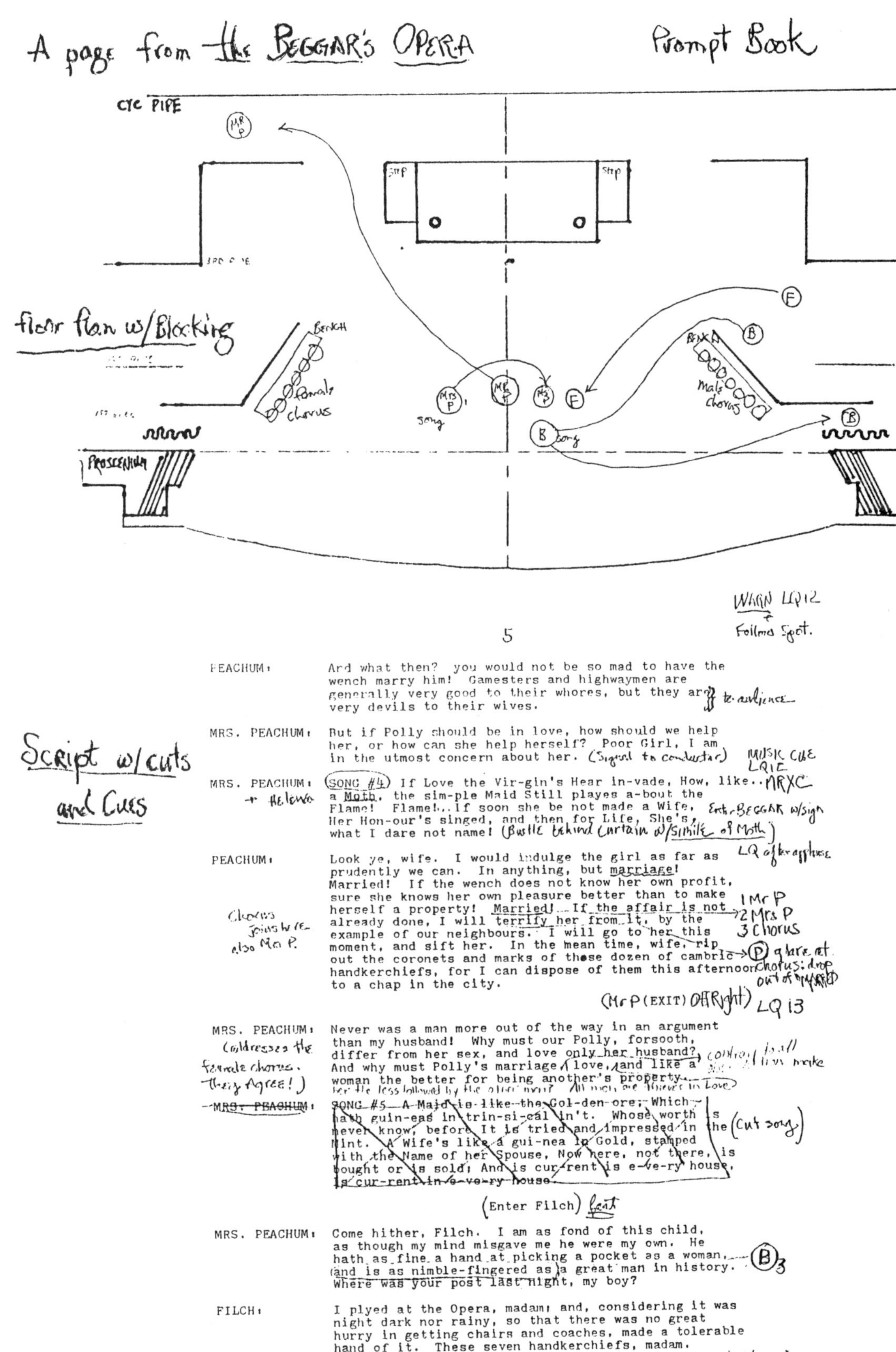
A page from the BEGGAR'S OPERA Prompt Book

Script w/cuts and Cues

WARN LQ 12 + Follow Spot.

5

PEACHUM: And what then? you would not be so mad to have the wench marry him! Gamesters and highwaymen are generally very good to their whores, but they are very devils to their wives. (to audience)

MRS. PEACHUM: But if Polly should be in love, how should we help her, or how can she help herself? Poor Girl, I am in the utmost concern about her. (Signal to conductor) MUSIC CUE LQ 12

MRS. PEACHUM: + Helena (SONG #4) If Love the Vir-gin's Hear in-vade, How, like a Moth, the sim-ple Maid Still playes a-bout the Flame! Flame!..If soon she be not made a Wife, Her Hon-our's singed, and then for Life, She's, what I dare not name! (Bustle behind curtain w/simile of Moth) MRXC Enter BEGGAR w/sign LQ after applause

PEACHUM: Look ye, wife. I would indulge the girl as far as prudently we can. In anything, but marriage! Married! If the wench does not know her own profit, sure she knows her own pleasure better than to make herself a property! Married! If the affair is not already done, I will terrify her from it, by the example of our neighbours. I will go to her this moment, and sift her. In the mean time, wife, rip out the coronets and marks of these dozen of cambric handkerchiefs, for I can dispose of them this afternoon to a chap in the city. (Chorus joins here also Mr P.) 1 Mr P 2 Mrs P 3 Chorus (P) glare at chorus: drop out of ... (Mr P (EXIT) Off Right) LQ 13

MRS. PEACHUM: (addresses the female chorus. They Agree!) Never was a man more out of the way in an argument than my husband! Why must our Polly, forsooth, differ from her sex, and love only her husband? And why must Polly's marriage, love, and like a woman the better for being another's property. ... All men are thieves in Love.

~~MRS. PEACHUM: SONG #5 A Maid is like the Gol-den ore; Which hath guin-eas in-trin-si-cal in't. Whose worth is never know, before It is tried and impressed in the Mint. A Wife's like a gui-nea in Gold, stamped with the Name of her Spouse, Now here, now there, is bought or is sold; And is cur-rent is e-ve-ry house, is cur-rent in e-ve-ry house.~~ (Cut song)

(Enter Filch) Exit

MRS. PEACHUM: Come hither, Filch. I am as fond of this child, as though my mind misgave me he were my own. He hath as fine a hand at picking a pocket as a woman, ~~and is as nimble-fingered as~~ a great man in history. ~~Where was your post last night~~, my boy? (B)3

FILCH: I plyed at the Opera, madam; and, considering it was night dark nor rainy, so that there was no great hurry in getting chairs and coaches, made a tolerable hand of it. These seven handkerchiefs, madam. (pulls them out one at a time)

Costumer's Analysis + Work Charts

HEDDA GABLER — Henrik Ibsen Name: ____________

Date of play ________ Location ____________

setting ________________

Time that elapses in play between acts ____________

	age	occupation	status	personality	Script references	# costumes	costume color
Hedda							
George							
Aunt Juliana							
Mrs Elvsted							
Judge Brack							
Eilert Louborg							
Berta							

complete chart on another sheet of paper

Costume chart

	Act 1	Act 2	Act 3	Act 4
Hedda				
George				
Aunt J.				
Mrs. Elvsted				
Brock				
Eilert				
Berta				

COSTUME CHART
ANYTHING GOES

BECK

NAME	I, i	I, ii	I, iii	I, iv	I, v	I vi	I, vii	I viii	II, i	II ii	III iii
Billy	Blue suit, tie white hat	same	same		Sailor suit yellow tie			Sailor suit, womans hat chef hat + apron	tux tie shirt	shirt pants	china suit
Reno	wht suit, straw hat, skirt, blouse				yellow shorts sash wht. top	maroon dress + choker	same with scarf	white coat + derby - beard	black dress		china suit
angels (4)	striped tops, wht. skirts, BLK. shorts hats, gloves			orange tops orange hats blk shorts			pink dresses plume hats chokers	purple dress	white dress beads		pink dresses (veils) (capes)
whitney	grey suit + hat, RWB ascot		same					white coat, derby	tux, tie shirt		same
Bonnie	polka dot dress hat, gloves	[illegible]	orange dress orange hat	same			pink + BLK dress pink scarf		white dress beads	pink dress	pink dress scarf
Moon	derby, blk. shirt striped suit		same		same	Same				same	china suit
Harcourt	Red coat, blk Top + skirt, blk hat, scarf				green coat blk skirt + top green hat			Fur coat blk + wht hat	white dress blk coat same hat		same
Hope	jumper + dress gloves	white Halter dress			halter dress blue coat			halter dress	black dress	same	blk + wht dress — veil
Evelyn	hat, sox, knickers, red coat, red shirt, bow tie, glasses	black suit shirt, yellow ascot			blk + red sweater knickers + sox hat	undershirt, suit pants		blk suit purple ascot	tux, spats tie, vest		Same
chinamen	blk suits + hats										
Steward	white + blk dress		same			Same					
purser	white outfit bow tie, shirt				same			same			
Captain	blk coat, white pants, bow tie wht. hat, shirt							same			
chorus	red hats + scarves dresses										
Sailors	suits, blue ties										
Reporter	suit, hat, tie										
Cameraman	Suit, hat, tie										

ONDINE
#2
ONDINE
#1
ONDINE
#3
ONDINE
ACT I

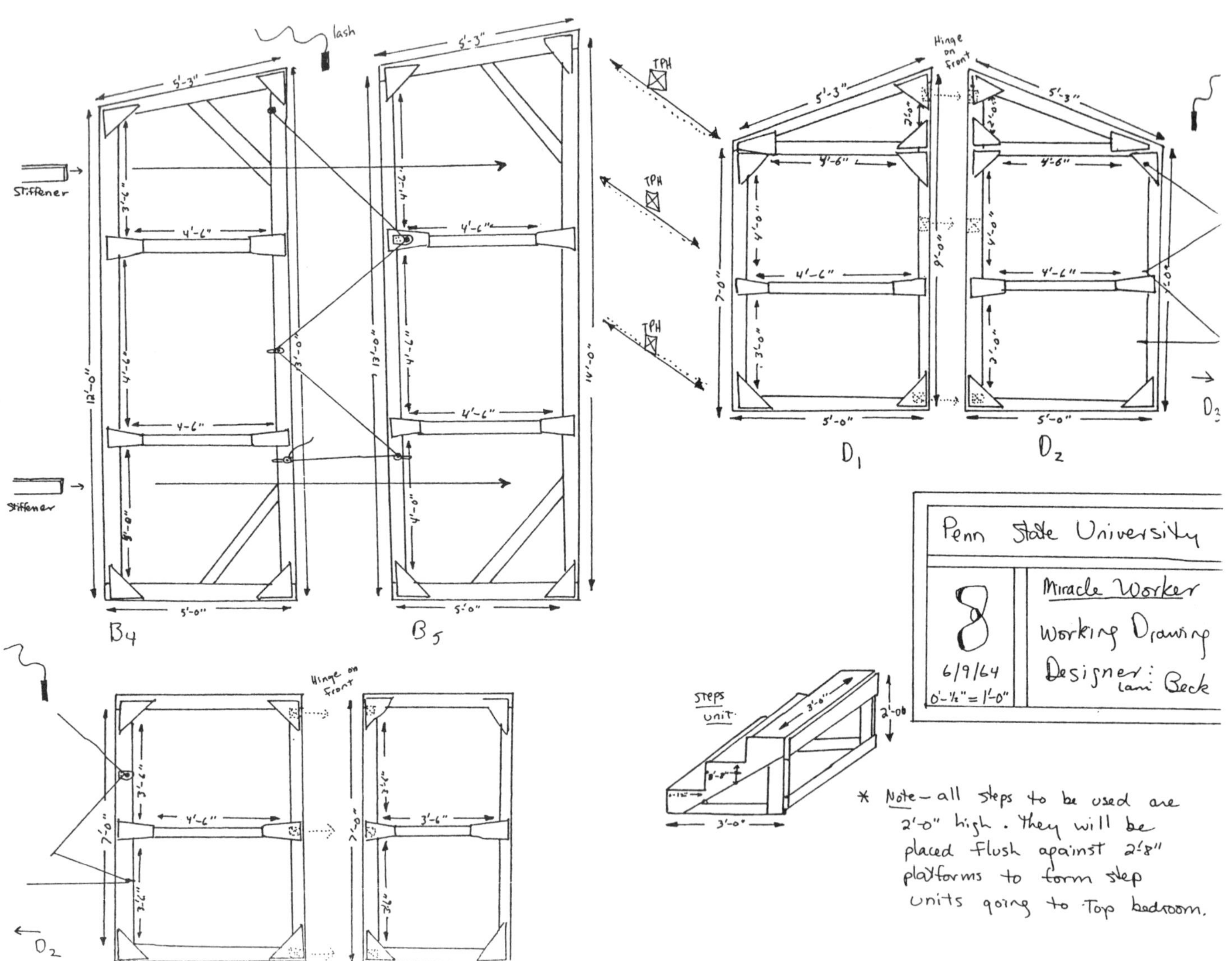

lash
Stiffener
Stiffener
B4
B5
TPH
TPH
TPH
Hinge on Front
D1
D2
Hinge on Front
O2
Steps unit
Penn State University
8
6/9/64
0'-½" = 1'-0"
Miracle Worker
Working Drawing
Designer: Lani Beck
* Note – all steps to be used are 2'-0" high. They will be placed flush against 2'-8" platforms to form step units going to Top bedroom.

INSTRUMENT	LAMP	COLOR	USE (AREA)	DIMMER	WATTS	COMMENTS
8" Leko	750	62	Area 11	1		2nd beam position
8" Leko	750	62	Area 11	1	2250	"
8" Leko	750	62	Area 11	1		"
8" Leko	750	29	Area 11	2		"
8" Leko	750	29	Area 11	2	2250	"
8" Leko	750	29	Area 11	2		"
16" Beam	1000	—	Area 11A	3	1000	" Special – Key ~ pump
8" Leko	750	54	Area 11 A	4	750	1st Beam position
8" Leko	750	29	Area 10	5	1500	
8" Leko	750	29	Area 1	5		
8" Leko	750	29	Area 2	6	1500	
8" Leko	750	29	Area 3	6		
8" Leko	750	29	Area 11A	7	750	
8" Leko	750	2	Area 10	8	1500	
8" Leko	750	2	Area 1	8		
8" Leko	750	2	Area 2	9	1500	
8" Leko	750	2	Area 3	9		
6" Fres	500	54	Area 4	10	1500	
6" Fres	500	54	Area 5	10		
6" Fres	500	54	Area 6	10		
8" Fres	500	29	Area 4	11		
6" Fres	500	29	Area 5	11	1500	
6" Fres	500	29	Area 6	11		
6" Fres	500	17	Area 9-10 (door)	12	500	Special – entrance under 8'-0" level
6" Fres	500	25	Area 9-10 (door)	13	500	" " " "
6" Fres	500	29	Area 9	14	500	
6" Fres	500	25	Area 8	15	1000	
6" Fres	500	25	Area 7	15		
6" Fres	500	29	Area 5-6 (Desk)	16	500	
6" Fres	500	62	Area 9	17	500	Special – desk
6" Fres	500	54	Area 5-6 (Desk)	18	500	Special – desk
6" Fres	500	54	Area 8	19		
8" Fres	1000	54	Special (table)	20 – 1000	1000	Barndoor – 4 way – table
6" Fres	500	54	Area 7	19		
6" Fres	500	41	Special	21	500	Back light for entrance
8" Fres	1000	21	Area 4	22	3000	
8" Fres	1000	21	Area 7	23		Backlights
8" Fres	1000	21	Area 5	22		
8" Fres	1000	21	Area 8	23	2000	
8" Fres	1000	21	Area 6	22		
8" Fres	1000	21	Area 9	24	1000	
8" Fres	1000	2	Area 4	25		
8" Fres	1000	2	Area 7	26		

Review Forms: Fill out the following for each play read or attended for this course.

1. Plot Sequence:

____

(Title of Play)

is the story of _______________________________________

(protagonist)

a(n) ____

(adj.) (adj.) (noun)

who because ____

(complication)

then sets out to ______________________________________

(action of play)

resulting in ____.

(resolution)

2. Theme: ____

____ .

3. Major Dramatic Question: ______________________________

____ ?

Answer: ____ .

4. Possible Metaphor: ___________________________________

____ .

Review Forms: Fill out the following for each play read or attended for this course.

1. Plot Sequence:

____

(Title of Play)

is the story of ____

(protagonist)

a(n) ____

(adj.) (adj.) (noun)

who because ____

(complication)

then sets out to ____

(action of play)

resulting in ____.

(resolution)

2. Theme: ____

____.

3. Major Dramatic Question: ____________________________________

____?

Answer: ____.

4. Possible Metaphor: ____

____.

Curtain Call!

There's nothing new in that old yarn:
We've got a show -- let's find a barn.
True talent can't stay dormant very long
It springs up all around us
like the chorus of a song.

Theatre, Theatre
        Just what is a theatre?
Look all around you and maybe you'll see it here.
Properties, costumes, scenery and things
Humanity's attic with left and right wings.

Theatre, Theatre
        Where can we find us one?
Listen for laughter, for applause and that kind of fun.
A hillside, an innyard, the most modest of space
Can expand to embrace the whole human race.

Theatre, Theatre
        Method or mimicry?
Humanity's artistic spirit is limit-free.
Everyone has a need for art to succeed
"To the Artist in us all!"   That's the theatre's creed.

Thaddeus L. Torp